HIDDEN BY THE DARK

A GRIPPING PSYCHOLOGICAL THRILLER
WITH A JAW-DROPPING TWIST (PINE
CREEK THRILLER BOOK 1)

J.C. MOORE

MISSINGSTARBOOKS

ISBN: 9798834386896

Cover Design by J.C. Moore

ALSO BY

Earth Rebels!: A Post Apocalyptic Survival Story
"Highly imaginative, intense, adventurous, and fun!"
- Reader Review
Aliens have invaded Earth and the fate of all humankind is not about an endless war against the countless hostile aliens and mutant species, but something far worse!
Death arenas, killer drones and new planets are only the beginning...
While they search for a new home - a new Earth, the few humans that have survived are fending for themselves in a hostile world.
Outnumbered and outgunned by the drones and human hunters sent by the Grey Ones, they must use all of their cunning and wits to survive.

One renegade fighter with an unlikely crew, and an aging ship the Avalon are all that stands between humanity and its destruction!

Ready for epic space battles, killer drones, and mutant species?

The Spirit Box

"What is the cost of greed? This is the question that The Spirit Box explores with terrifyingly good storytelling that pulls the reader into a chilling page turner of an offering that was a true joy to read! - Bravo" - Reader Review

One man's obsession with power and wealth leads him to the Spirit Box where the dead will promise these things - with a cost.

The dead will want what is theirs.

And so, it waited, always ready to consume them. The dead are very patient they will wait for their moment with their gifts for the living.

PRAISE FOR HIDDEN BY THE DARK

"I loved this. A touch of spooky with mystery. A must have." *Amazon Reviewer*

"It is a well written story with a good hook. Keeps you reading until the end. Good read." *Amazon Reviewer*

"This author does not leave anything out. There are such vivid descriptions and there is an equal balance between dark and light in them. This dark tale shows us that horror can transcend the genre as well." *Amazon Reviewer*

"I found this title while searching for authors similar to Stephen King. I thought I would give it a try. Very well written, and the story is thoughtful. Great murder mystery!" *Amazon Reviewer*

"This was a great book. I love the fact that it had

me in suspense through-out the entire read." *Amazon Reviewer*

J.C. MOORE AUTHOR

Get Sci-Fi And Horror and free stories in your inbox! Also, the occasional short story *sent free* - just for subscribing.
Visit jcmooreauthor.com
Facebook
https://www.facebook.com/jcmooreauthor
Instagram
https://www.instagram.com/jcmoorewrites/
Goodreads
https://www.goodreads.com/johnm53

CONTENTS

To my parents-
For taking the time to make glorious memories in the hills of West Virginia as a kid.

Yea, though I walk through the valley of the shadow of death, I will fear no evil: for thou art with me; thy rod and thy staff they comfort me...

Psalms 23:4

ONE

Tightening his hands into fists, he forced himself to push his fingers until they formed a steeple. His face was tense, and he felt the tension of the situation make itself known. This was more than death, more than a murder scene. This was the work of a madman, out of his mind with rage, maddened to the point of insanity from inner demons. *Another mutilated body was found here in our town!* He had seen death before, but not like this.

He let out a long breath as if he had been holding it for hours. Finally, he released the tension and brought his palms together, squeezing his hands between his knees. He had taught this gesture to himself years ago as a way of calming down during stressful situations. Over the years, he had forgotten about it and now, in this moment of despair, it arrived like the return of an old friend. His hands pressed against his legs for several moments until he filled the silence with a return to normal breathing.

The whole town would demand answers and justice. People were tired of the disappearances, tired of the lack of answers, and tired of having to worry about their loved ones. He opened his eyes, hoping that the situation was not what it seemed. On the wall across from his desk hung a picture of him and his wife when they were young.

She had been gone for fifteen years now, taking that part of his life with her, as well as a part of him. He thought about how strange it was that such a big part of her life had passed since she died, and he moved on with his own. The picture on the wall showed him looking at a smiling woman in a pink dress. She leaned against him, and he wrapped a protective arm around her shoulders. The happiness on their faces was almost tangible like it was possible to reach out and touch it. She had worn pink that day because he loved it on her, and because this was their wedding day.

He searched his heart for something that would let him draw from the well of his youth and strength. There was nothing.

But then he remembered. He had to do the job. He had a duty to the town, a duty to his family. His son was also dead, but he had a duty to preserve the memory of him. He cracked the knuckles of both hands, feeling them bleed underneath scaly red skin.

He stood and walked to the window. He knew his deputy could not manage this case on her own.

Every week, he brought in people to the station for domestic violence and assaults, and he always thought the same thing: "This town is going to explode." It was his job to make sure it didn't. He had been a police officer in this

2

town for twenty years and had never wavered from his duty. Now was no different, except that if he failed, he himself would be responsible for everything that happened next.

I won't let that happen, he thought. He walked over to his chair and sat down.

The killer would strike again; he knew it. He did not want to be the sheriff of a town where people were afraid to let their loved ones out of their sight. He knew that if anyone found out about another murder, the town would be in a frenzy of fear, blame, and accusation. Something had to be done, but what? For every action there is an equal and opposite reaction, he thought. He needed to do something about the situation, and he needed to make it count.

The intercom buzzed. "Sheriff, I'm getting calls about the body."

He hung up the phone and walked over to the large window behind his desk. The parking lot was empty except for the patrol car. He saw it and imagined someone sitting in the driver's seat with the windows rolled up, the radio playing, and a cigarette dangling from the corner of their mouth. When he was a child, he would sit in his room, staring out of his window. He'd imagine what was going on in the rest of town. He'd look at the things he could see, and he'd imagine what he couldn't see. As he got older, though, he looked at things differently. He imagined things that weren't there. There were places that didn't exist that he filled in the blanks with. He imagined love where there was only hate, and he imagined hate where there was only love.

It was an odd thing because it seemed as if he were the only person in the world who'd ever experienced it. He wondered if he was normal, but he shrugged the thought away. He was perfectly normal. It was just that his experience differed from other people's experiences.

He turned from the window and looked at the pictures on his wall. The photographs captured brief moments of his life: The first time he went skydiving, his son's graduation, a hike with a couple of friends through Hong Kong's mountains, and a picture of his wife taken one night as she was sleeping beside him. He had all these little snapshots of beautiful moments to remind him that life was amazing.

As a child, he would look at the pictures of his father in uniform. He would look at the pictures of his mother with her friends and with her kids, or the pictures of his father in uniform with his friends. He was always trying to figure things out. When he was young, he thought he could just ask questions. When he got older, he knew he had to find answers.

When he got older still, he knew he had to make sure the answers he got were correct. He had to make sure that he never fell into the same trap as his father. So, he made sure he didn't.

Five years sober now, he could admit it. He wasn't sure how he had gotten there; he wasn't sure how he made it work. But he knew he was in trouble. He knew he was obsessed with the idea of a drink. He counted seconds, minutes, and hours to keep his head off the drink. When people asked him what time it was, he laughed and could tell them without looking at his wrist. He knew he could turn back into a drunk. All he had to do was take that first drink. He knew it wouldn't take too much. Just that bit of nip to get his taste buds working.

The door opened behind him, and he turned around to see his deputy walk into his office. Her hand was on the butt of her gun, and she looked ready to take on all comers. Her brown hair was pulled into a tight ponytail, and strands of it had escaped, hanging across her cheeks. She wore jeans, a flannel shirt, and cowboy boots. She was young, and she carried herself like she was in charge. A pistol was strapped to her waist, and he could tell she was itching to use it. He doubted she had ever shot a human being, but he could see the hint of a restless spirit lurking beneath the surface of her mind.

"What's going on, Sheriff?" she said.

The sheriff turned around and looked out at the parking lot again. It was Deputy Madison Colby. She paced back and forth, hands in her pockets. She showed no outward sign of anxiety, but he knew she was nervous from her body language. He had seen people take on this same arrogant stance hundreds of times. He had detained plenty of people during his career, and he had sent his share of people to jail. He had even sent a few people to death row, though the state no longer used the death penalty.

"Joel Gabriel was found dead and mutilated in Pencenpau Park."

By now, the reporters and camera crews had joined the group, their numbers multiplying like bacteria.

The air thickened with questions: "Why are you here? Is it a murder? The coroner says so. Who found the body? I

5

didn't know he was missing... I saw him yesterday. Who is the victim?" Each one sounded louder than the last, like a chorus of cicadas on a summer night. The questions swirled through the air like autumn leaves, blown along by a gust of wind.

He bit the words apart, making each one sharp and hard. "I was at the crime scene this morning."

"It was Joel?" Her voice quivered.

"Yes. It's a horrible mess," he said. He shook his head. The lines on his brow deepened. "The coroner will find out what happened, I'm sure of it."

"Why would someone want to kill old Joel? It makes little sense. There wasn't a person in Pine Creek who wouldn't consider him a friend." She paced the room, wringing her hands.

"It could have been a robbery gone wrong, though," the sheriff said. His voice was soft, choked with emotion. "He's got more gold than most folks in these parts." His brown eyes locked on hers, fierce with determination.

"That might have made him a target." He sighed and pressed his hands together between his knees. "It also may be a serial murder," he continued after he had composed himself.

"I was thinking that."

He cut her off. "I'm not sure if this has anything to do with those missing people, but I want to keep things quiet. I know you have a life of your own, but this case is going to require our full attention. The department is shorthanded, anyway. I don't think anyone will notice."

Shaking her head, she frowned. "Sheriff, we've talked about this before. I'm not a rookie anymore. We've worked together for over two years now."

"I'm trying to be nice here, Madison. I'm trying to put you in a position where you can succeed."

She snorted. "I'm not a failure. I'm a damn good cop."

The sheriff stared hard at her, eye to eye. He held his gaze steady, locking eyes with her until she looked away.

"You're right. You are fantastic at what you do, but you are young. I need you to trust me. You might not realize it now, but this case is going to require us to work together."

"What do you mean by that?"

"I mean, I'm going to have my hands full, and I'm going to need you to help me with things that aren't the most important part of the case."

"You mean the media and the public?" Madison said.

He nodded. "That's why I need you to keep things quiet. You know what the press is like. You know what the public wants to hear. I need you to keep them happy."

She turned back to the room and crossed to the window. "The town is going to want retribution."

"They are. That's why we need to solve this case quickly. This isn't a regular murder. This was Joel Gabriel. A husband, and father of three, devoted to the church and to his community and business. He had more going for him than almost anyone in this town." the sheriff paused and ran a hand through his hair. "It was brutal."

He sighed as he continued. "I mean, there could be more to this than just one person killing another person. It could end up being worse."

7

"Worse? How much worse can you get? What is it?" she asked.

He shook his head and tossed his phone onto the desk.

"I don't know." His voice was dark with worry.

"This place is small and peaceful, yet a man was killed in the middle of town. His hands were bound, and his body was dragged through the woods, mutilated, and thrown away like a piece of trash onto the side of the road where it was found by someone who was headed out to his mailbox."

"That's horrible." she gasped.

"Yes, it is."

"This could be someone from out of town."

"I'm sure the killer is from town. If he wasn't, there would be more than one murder to deal with."

"Maybe it's the same person who took those missing people and killed that bartender? We still never found who killed her."

"That's what I'm afraid of." he concurred.

"Then what do you think it is?"

"I don't know. I don't want to jump to any conclusions yet. We need to see Walker and have him give us the coroner's report," he said.

She nodded. "Right now?"

"Right now."

They crossed to the door, and the sheriff locked it. He slid the bolt into the latch, placing the key into his pocket.

Taking his hat off the peg, he slipped on his jacket and turned to his deputy.

"You ready?"

She nodded, and they stepped out into the parking lot. The parking lot was cobblestone, surrounded by a low, wrought-iron fence. A police cruiser sat in the center of the courtyard. Getting into the car, he started the engine. They drove through the streets of the small town. The sheriff drove slowly. His eyes scanned his surroundings as he drove by the shops and stores that lined the way. He was watching for signs of trouble, suspicious activity, or hostile intent. He was paying attention to who was watching them and who was pretending not to notice their presence.

He said, "There's something strange about this town."

"What do you mean?"

"I mean, I feel like I'm missing something. I feel like there's something I don't know."

She nodded. She said nothing for a long time. They drove for a few miles, and he eventually turned the car down a side street that led through the trees and down into the valley. A green canopy of leaves, thick and fragrant, over-hung the road and dappled the sunlight with shadows and light. The trees grew thicker, their trunks close together, blocking any light from reaching the forest floor. The road was so overgrown with grasses and vines that it became impossible to know how wide or narrow it had once been.

They drove further until they reached a small clearing on the side of the road. A few cars, some old and some new were parked on the gravel, and there was a sign for the little town's cemetery. He turned onto the side road, and they followed it back into the woods. Driving down into the valley, they passed under a big sign that read:

Pine Creek Memorial, Funeral Home, And Clean Cremation Services

Beyond that, there was a cream-colored gate with scroll-work curlicues surrounding it. In the distance, the sheriff noticed a tall mausoleum with a red-tiled roof and an open portico surrounded by pillars.

He made a right turn and drove up a long driveway. Tall trees and shrubs lined the road, shielding the old stone and mortar buildings from passing motorists. The sheriff looked out over the buildings that were clustered down the far end of the road. Trees and bushes separated them, and he saw a sign for the coroner's office. His heart skipped a beat. He drove past the buildings and noticed one that had a sign, "Parking." He pulled into an empty parking space labeled "Sheriff" and popped the car door open.

"That's it." He lifted a calloused finger and pointed toward a small building with a peaked, shingled roof and diamond-paned windows. "Right there."

They stepped out of the car. As they were about to make their way inside, the pair passed a man leaning against the wall, his mouth holding a cigarette that had burned down until the end was a tiny nub. He took a long drag and then dropped the cigarette, grinding it under his boot.

Raising his eyebrows, the man looked directly at the sheriff. "It's not even noon, and you're here."

The sheriff nodded. "That's right."

"I didn't call you."

"No, you didn't."

The tall, wide man looked into the sheriff's eyes. An intense feeling of dread immediately came over the sheriff.

The man's large hands and knuckles, covered with liver spots and circular red spots with clear borders, the remnants of pustules that had healed long ago, clutched a vinyl bag. The man's face was wide, with a smooth and wrinkled forehead dominated by small and deep-set eyes. They were like the eyes of a wild cave-dwelling animal, a bear, or a wolf, searching for prey with slightly insane light.

Walker James had just received the body a few hours earlier. He'd been in the middle of a routine procedure when the call came in. A small town like Pine Creek rarely received a dead body, especially a murder case. Several months earlier, a hiker found a mutilated body. The same coroner had been called for that one, and they didn't release the details. The autopsy had been quick, and they sent the body to the medical examiner in a nearby town.

The body that came in today bothered him. He had seen a lot of deaths in his day, but none like this. It was the sheer brutality of it, especially to an older man that always kept to himself, and the community loved him. This death had been no accident. The cruelty of it was enough to bother him, but what bothered him, even more, was how this death affected the town itself. Who had done this? What monsters lived here that they could do something like this?

The sheriff pointed to the coroner's office. "You ready to give me the report?"

Walker nodded, and the two men went inside.

Madison followed behind them, closing the door behind her. The air inside the building was quiet. It smelled of dust and mold. The walls were covered with drywall, and a few giant pieces of furniture were pushed up against a wall. A brightly lit hallway led to a long corridor that disappeared around a corner.

A door shut behind her. There was another door ahead of her, which led to a sparsely furnished room.

The men disappeared around a corner and a door closed behind them. Madison stood at the closed door and stared at the wall.

She heard the deep voice of the sheriff.

"I want to know everything. Everything I've got to know."

"You don't want me to sugar-coat it?"

"Sugar-coat it?"

"Yeah, you know, soften the blow. Make it seem better than it is."

"No, I want you to tell me everything. Just tell me. Don't worry about me. Tell me exactly what you found." the sheriff said.

Madison pulled out her phone and checked the screen. No messages. She stepped back from the door and had a seat in an old wooden chair. The seat was dusty, and her new black slacks were probably ruined by now, but she didn't care that much. She sneezed as she sat down in it. She pulled her pant legs up over her shoes and folded her hands. The muffled voice of the sheriff drifted through the walls like sunlight through glass.

"All right then, I'll tell you what I found. I'll tell you what I know."

"That's all I want from you, Walker."

She walked into the morgue where Walker stood over a white slab that was covered with a sheet. He looked to his left and saw Madison standing by the doorway. The sheriff was standing behind him, leaning against the wall with his arms crossed. Walker raised an eyebrow, and Madison nodded.

"It's okay" the sheriff reassured him.

"Alright then, there's not a whole lot to tell. The knife nicked the sternum and edges of the rib cage twice. They gutted him from the navel to the groin. Small puncture wounds over the entire body. The flesh was carefully cut and peeled away from the bone, but nothing was taken. The organs were left to spill out across the cane field. We found him here, face down, with a knife sticking from his spine. There's no blood on or around him. I mean none. Not a single drop."

"I don't understand that."

"You got me. There's no trace of it. I mean, it's not like the killer took some blood and wiped the knife off, because there's no trace of the blood on the knife or around the wound. It's like the body bled on the ground and then it just... disappeared."

Madison sighed. She took a step toward the doctor.

"What about the weapon?" she asked.

He shook his head. "It was just a regular kitchen knife. Nothing special about it. The blade was new, but that's about it."

Madison looked over at the sheriff. "Did you find anything at the scene?"

The sheriff shook his head. "Nothing. Just a few manilla envelopes, but they were empty. Just print dust."

Madison went back to the wall and leaned against it. "Shit."

"Well, we must work with it. I'll have the evidence team search for stray prints and see if they can find any trace of the blood."

"That's all I can tell you."

"How long was he like that?"

"I don't know. I mean, there were no flies on the body, so I don't think he was there too long. The body was in good condition. Muscle rigor had started to set in, but he wasn't as stiff as he should have been."

She nodded.

"I'm going to need you to do a full workup. I want a complete autopsy and toxicology," The sheriff demanded.

"Shouldn't you wait for his family?" Walker responded.

"Wait for the family?"

"Yeah, shouldn't you wait for the family before you do an autopsy?"

"The family will have to wait for the autopsy. It's just that simple."

Walker nodded. "I'll get started then."

He turned away from her as he started unhooking the straps that held the body to the table.

Madison looked at the body. She didn't want to see it with the flesh all mangled. It looked wrong.

The sheriff walked up to her and put a hand on her shoulder.

"I know this is hard," the sheriff said, "but we have to get moving." He looked at her and pressed his lips together.

"I know," she responded

"We will find who did this," the sheriff spoke.

"Good. Let me know if you need anything." Walker said with a smile.

She nodded, and the men walked away, leaving her alone with the body. She stared at it for a moment and wondered about the how and why.

Why had the body been left on the ground like that? How had the killer gotten it from the house to the cane field?

She looked up at the ceiling. The air was heavy with dust and decaying matter. The fluorescent light buzzed and flickered above her head, and she took a step toward the body.

It was a gruesome death. She could tell that he had been alive, probably begging for his life, as the killer cut him open and removed his organs, one by one.

A gust of air blew through the room, and it carried a dusty smell with it.

She heard a voice behind her.

"I want to know everything. Just tell me."

She turned around and saw the sheriff standing in the doorway.

"You got it."

Madison stared at the body for a moment longer. She turned away from the table and followed the sheriff back to his office.

They got back into their patrol car and drove to the office in silence. Madison tried to shake off the chill that was sucking the life out of her. All she could think about was why? Why would anyone do something like that? She had spent three years in the academy because she wanted to protect and serve, and she would do nothing less than everything she could think of to find answers for the families of this small town.

A gust of wind blew down the street. The naked branches groaned and creaked. Sunlight filtered through the leaves, casting a golden aura on the fallen leaves, looking like golden coins as they fluttered to the ground. A few thin voices crept through the cracks in the pavement, calling to her. A blast of wind from the north rushed into the parking lot. The orange and yellow leaves quivered and shook, sending a chorus of color into the air. Like giant cymbals clashing, the branches rattled the windows and made the ground shake. She turned away from the window and looked at the sheriff.

"Are you alright?" she asked.

"I'm fine."

He slowed down and turned onto the main road and sped up.

"Do you have any ideas?"

He shook his head once, keeping his eyes on the road. "Not really, but I'll find out what happened. I promise you that."

"Do you think he was targeted?"

He shrugged slightly and kept looking at the road. "No idea. That's not what happens around here."

"Tell me about it."

"I've lived here all my life. It's a bit of a quiet town. There's the occasional bar fight, but that's about it."

"I'm sure it's not that quiet."

"Yeah, well, you get used to it."

He reached over and turned on the radio. A song was in full swing. It was country, with clear, twangy vocals and a solid bass line played by a steel guitar. The sheriff started tapping his hand against the steering wheel to the beat of the song. The singer's voice was sullen, like that of a man who had been broken by love's deception. He would be lost without his love, no matter how much it hurt to remember her. *"My heart can't take it,"* he sang, *"When you ain't here to hold."*

She had lived in several small towns, and every single one of them had a classic country station. Soft guitars, fiddles, and basses played bluegrass music in a minor key. The songs sounded like advertisements for a place that didn't really exist. She sighed, and the sheriff looked over at her. He had a gentle face and eyes the color of warm chocolate.

"Is something wrong?" he asked.

"No."

"I mean, I don't mean to be insensitive or anything, but you seem like you're in a bad mood," he continued.

She shrugged. "I just don't like this case."

"Yeah, it's a damn shame."

"I mean, if he was killed by a burglar, I wouldn't have a problem with it, but why was he gutted like that? Why go through all that trouble to kill him?"

The sheriff looked up at the sky and shrugged.

"I don't know. I mean, if it makes you feel any better, I don't think he knew whoever killed him."

"How do you know?"

"Because I knew the man, and he didn't strike me as the type who would make enemies."

17

Madison sighed and looked out the window. "I don't like it."

The white building was an oasis in the small Southern town. A short, covered porch with rocking chairs sat off to one side, like a grandmother sitting at her front window, watching to make sure the children were behaving.

They parked in the parking lot and walked up the stone steps leading to the office. The sheriff sat behind his desk and took a deep breath. Stacked up by his computer was a small pile of papers, not yet organized into neat piles with rubber bands around them. He leaned back in his chair and put his feet on his desk. Madison sat down in the chair opposite him, in front of his desk, unsure if there were customs or rules, she hadn't learned yet.

He took a deep breath and rubbed his hand against his face. "Tell me what you know."

Madison nodded and leaned back in her chair.

"The victim was found outside of his home by his neighbors. His body was in the cane field behind his property. There was blood on the ground, but there was no trace of it on the body or around his body. There were a few envelopes on the ground as well, but they were empty."

He shook his head. "Sounds like a robbery gone wrong."

"I don't know. I mean, it could be, but what would have been the point of that?"

The sheriff, a naturally big man, leaned forward and looked at her with his big brown eyes, which had an extra bit of shine behind them.

"Seriously?"

"Seriously, what?"

"You don't think that a robbery could have gone wrong?"

"No, I mean, yeah, it could have, but why would he have been outside of his home at night? He didn't know the burglar. Why would he have opened the door?"

"Maybe he was going to the bathroom."

"He didn't have anything on him. No wallet, no money, no watch, no phone. Nothing that would indicate that he was even walking outside to piss."

"Maybe he forgot something." he countered.

"And he got butchered for it?"

"Maybe someone wanted to rob him, and it just got out of hand."

"Then why go through all the trouble of taking out his organs?"

"I don't know."

Madison shook her head.

"It doesn't make sense." She spoke.

"What about the neighbors? Did they see anything?"

"Yeah, but they aren't talking. They think it's a curse."

The sheriff looked up at the smoke alarm, which had beeped, and took out the battery to silence it.

A smile played on his lips, and a leer wrinkled his hairy cheeks.

"I know it sounds crazy. They say that the devil is walking through the woods. Ever since the accident at the coal mines happened many years back."

"What?"

"The devil. They say the devil is walking through the woods, haunting these hills."

There had been a terrible accident at the coal mines years before trapping miners underground. The rescue efforts had been too slow. Only three miners had survived. She remembered reading about the rescue on the paper and seeing the grainy and dark photographs of the men standing around in the crisp uniforms of the mining company. She knew they were watching their friends and fellow miners die. Some people believed that they may have dug too far. They had cut corners, or maybe they were just trying to make a little more money.

She remembered her father had told her that men do not dig holes in the ground because they love to dig holes. They do it because they need the money. There were two things in life he knew for certain: no one dug a hole unless they had to, and there was no such thing as a rich miner.

She had always heard that there were mines as far back as anyone could remember. The people who first settled in the area had first dug them out, but now, sadly, it was a dying industry. The mines would close and never reopen, and one day they would fill the hole in, and it would be just a hole in the ground again.

Leaning back in her chair, she could feel the smooth leather against her hands. She looked at the sky outside her window. A flock of birds soared across the wide expanse of blue. It was an afternoon like any other in the autumn, when long hours of sunlight were interspersed with sudden storms. The row of trees, covered in brown leaves, cast a long shadow on the fields, which had turned golden and yellow under the late summer sun. The view was calming and familiar.

"Wait a minute, a devil in the woods?"

"Yeah. Why?"

Madison uncrossed her legs, lifted her arms off the back of her chair, and leaned forward. Her shoulders rose and her nostrils flared, widening her already large nose. She closed her eyes and sighed, drawing a deep breath through her nostrils.

The sheriff rubbed his eyes and looked over at Madison. A frown twisted her face into a knot of confusion. "I don't believe in devils," Madison stated.

"Neither do I," the sheriff replied. They were both silent for a moment. The minute hand on the clock scraped the last second and moved on to the next minute. It continued to tick as the sheriff leaned forward, his hands and elbows on the table. He sighed loudly.

"You know, I never believed in that devil, either. I mean, it's one thing for my mom to tell me about it, but it's another thing to see it for myself."

"What do you mean?" Madison asked.

"Well, when I was a kid, my mom would tell me about the devil that was walking through the woods. She would tell me that if I left the house at night and wandered out into the woods, I'd see the devil with my own eyes."

"And did you?"

"No, of course not. I mean, obviously I wouldn't wander out into the woods at night."

"Why not?"

"Why not? Because it's dangerous. It's dangerous to wander out there during the day, too, but at night it's even worse. There are bears, and panthers, and God knows what else is out there."

"Why would you believe in it?"

"It was my mother's fault. She would always tell me stories when I was a kid about the devil roaming the woods. She would tell me about the devil and the souls of the damned, which then became a part of me."

"Parents and their superstitions." she sighed.

"Yeah. You know, I always thought it was bullshit, though."

Madison laughed, her rich voice radiating through the room.

The sheriff leaned back in his chair, which creaked loudly. He looked around his corner table and sighed. What would his mother think if she knew he was talking to a girl like Madison? He imagined her sitting in her rocking chair on the porch of their house back home, shaking her head with disapproval.

He remembered how he would look up at his mother, furrowing his brows, his eyes wide and questioning.

"I'm surprised you believed in it." She spoke.

"Yeah, I'm easily swayed. I mean, my mother is an old woman. Her logic is shaky, and she is prone to exaggeration. I guess I believed it despite that."

She looked back at him. Her eyes were enormous and round, like those of a doe, when it expects hunters to appear at any moment. They were the color of the sky, just as the sun hit it. Her skin was fair, almost white. Her hair was a deep brown in stark contrast to her skin tone. She had full lips and a smile that was close to the shape of her face. The lipstick that she wore was a pleasing contrast to the rest of her hair and face.

"What are you thinking?" she asked.

"I'm thinking that I need to find out more about the victim."

"You mean the body?"

The sheriff leaned forward and scratched the back of his neck. "No, I mean the victim."

Madison furrowed her brows, and a look of confusion washed over her face. "What do you mean?"

"I mean, I need to find more information about the victim; about who he is and what he was doing, instead of focusing on the body."

"I'm not sure I understand."

"Yeah, I know it sounds crazy, but it's the only way to see if this was a robbery or if this was a murder. I need to find out who the victim was and why he was killed. Because if I don't know that, then I don't know who did it."

She sighed and nodded. "Maybe. What are you going to do?"

The sheriff stood up and walked across the room to the counter by the fridge. Its white paint had yellowed with age and cracked with sun-faded corners. He opened the door with a click, peeled back the rust-speckled handle, pulled out two bottles of water, and brought them over to the table. He set one down in front of her and took a seat again.

She hadn't realized how hot she had gotten during their conversation.

"Thank you." She unscrewed the cap and took a sip.

"We have to dig deeper into witnesses and suspects. Maybe find a piece of gold that slipped through the cracks the first time. A new angle."

He took a swig of the water and sat it back down on the table. "Most people don't want to get involved. Most people take the path of least resistance. They don't always want to talk"

"You're right about most people." She took another gulp. The cool liquid ran down her throat, quenching her thirst almost instantly.

"We need to find someone who is the opposite of most people."

"Like who?"

"We need to find a witness with a reason to talk."

Madison was exhausted and wanted to go home and get some rest.

"You're right. You're right." She stood up. "I'll see you tomorrow. I am beat."

"Hold on." He got up, came around the table, and hugged her. "I don't know where we would be without you," he whispered.

"Why do you say that?" She blushed.

"Because we would have had to bring in a brand-new deputy to take over for me in homicide. No one wants that job because there's such a stigma attached to it. They're afraid they'll never get out of it. You stepped right up."

"Oh," she whispered in response, her voice rising.

"You've been a real trooper, Madison."

"Now, go home and get some rest. You're going to need it. I'll talk to you in the morning about the case."

She loosened the tie around her collar, pulled it into her hands, and tossed it onto the desk. She turned and walked out of the room. The carpet swished under her feet as she walked. She strolled down the hallway and out into the parking lot. Popping the trunk of her car, she placed her bag inside.

She pressed her hand onto the gearshift, the cool surface sinking into the heat of her palm. She released the clutch and pushed on the gas, watching it rise from its resting place. The engine roared to life, shaking the car, and rumbling in her chest. It was a deep, throaty bellow. She pressed the gas pedal down, then released it and tore out of the parking lot as she drove away from the sheriff's office.

She pulled into her driveway. The moon was full and hung low in the sky. It gleamed off the hood of her car and cast a soft white light on her face. She climbed the steps to her front porch, unlocked the door, and walked inside. The apartment was dark, but she knew the way by heart. She walked over to the kitchen, opened the fridge, and took out a leftover chicken breast and some lettuce. She dropped the chicken in a bowl, put it in some water, and let it defrost in the fridge.

She turned off the kitchen light that cast a dim yellow glow into the living room and walked past her favorite chair. Pulling the blinds down over the bay window, she walked through the dark to the bathroom. She turned on the bright light in the bathroom and pulled off her sweater and shirt, looking at her smooth skin under the lights. She looked at her body in the mirror and turned on the water. It rushed out of the faucet, hot, then cold, then hot again.

Then she looked in the mirror and saw her blue eyes staring back at her. Her wet hair clung to her skin like seaweed. She weighed her options and turned around to grab the whisky from the bed. The neck of the bottle was corked, and she struggled to get it off. A stab was no good; she needed a saw. After leaving the room, she went into the kitchen to open her utensil drawer. She found a carving knife and sat it on the counter before walking back into the bathroom. She picked up the whisky and set it on the sink. Grabbing a washcloth from the rack, she wet it with warm water, wrung it out, and washed her face. Then she dried it, brushed off her shoulders, and grabbed her phone so she could call her mom back. She dialed her mother's number and listened to the rings on the other end of the line. Tears rolled down her face as she listened to her mother's voicemail greeting. She left a voicemail in return.

She ran the knife over her face and let the water sluice off the soap, watching it disappear into the drain. She then scrubbed out her mouth and spat into the drain. The water was hot, too hot for her to take more than a couple of minutes under it. She turned off the water and climbed back out of the shower. She walked back into the bedroom.

Sitting down on the bed, she looked at the bottle of scotch sitting on the floor. She picked it up and tried to read the label in the dim light. She put it back down and looked around for her bag, finding it underneath a pile of clothes on a chair by the door of the bedroom. It was made of stiff cloth, with a wide strap along its length so she could wear it across her chest like a satchel. She pulled it close to her and dug around in it until she found what she was looking for.

She pulled out a big silver Zippo and flicked it straight. A small flame popped out of the top with a hiss, and she pressed it up against the cigarette in her mouth. She inhaled and let the smoke fill her lungs, holding it there for a few seconds before she exhaled a cloud of white smoke. She took another drag, held it, and released it. Before she knew it, she'd already finished half the cigarette. She took another drag and pulled the cigarette out of her mouth. The cherry was a hot coal in the dim light. She let it sit there for a second and then flicked it into the ashtray on her nightstand. Reaching into the bag again, she pulled out another cigarette and lit it. She took a drag and held it in her lungs, then exhaling slowly. She put the cigarette back in her mouth and tapped the hot coal into the ashtray then taking a final drag. The cigarette continued to glow. Flicking the butt into the ashtray again, she watched it burn and eventually fizzle into the darkness.

Two

"Dad," she asked, "are you sure there's no more cereal in the box?"

"Yes, dear, there is. I just poured you some. Here you go." he said.

"Thanks."

"No problem."

The soft clink of a spoon against a ceramic bowl and the slurping sound of her eating cereal filled the room.

Jenny was rushing to get ready for school. She was pouring cereal into her bowl and then scraping the sides to get all the milk. The hectic morning routine was never-ending. There was always something that had to be done, and it was up to her to take care of everything. It felt like she was never getting enough sleep. She was always tired and had to go to bed early, but then she always woke up late.

She was rushing to get dressed and get to school on time. The last thing she wanted was to get to school late. If she was always late, she didn't know if she could make friends. She wouldn't have time to talk to them.

Jumping into her car, she pulled out of the driveway. It was freezing outside, and she hadn't even noticed it until now. She didn't know if she should roll up her windows or turn on the heater.

Her vision was blurry, and she could barely make out what was in front of her. She should have gone to bed earlier; she was so tired it felt like she hadn't slept at all. Her body finally registered the rough surface under her fingers, which she knew well from handling it so often before.

Her battered black car rolled to a stop in front of the high school. Her friend Meg was standing by her car holding her bag. The strands of Meg's dark hair framed her face in lacquered layers, laying in a neat line across her shoulders. Jenny stepped out of the car. A hint of a smile played across Meg's lips, her eyes crinkling in merriment. In a smooth voice, which held just a hint of edge and gravel, she asked, "So, what did you do this weekend?"

"Nothing," said Jenny. Her voice was flat with annoyance. "It was kind of boring."

"What did you do on Friday?" Meg pressed.

"I hung out with my brother, but then I had to go right to bed."

"Did you do anything fun?"

"There was this party on Friday night. I thought it would be fun, but it sucked—everyone was drunk, and a bunch of fights broke out. They ended up calling the cops." Jenny rolled her eyes.

"Are you making that up?"

"You don't believe me?"

Meg wore red lipstick and black eyeliner. Her eyes were green. She was tanned, and her skin looked tight against her silver T-shirt. The tattoo of a daisy on her shoulder danced in the sunlight. Her silver bracelets clinked together as she fidgeted. She spoke with an Italian accent. She wore denim shorts and sneakers with lime green laces.

But Jenny had on a pair of Levi's that hugged her hips like a second skin and a crisp button-up shirt that was off white, stitched with red thread to form a design Meg couldn't quite make out. The shirt was studiously clean and pressed but looked a bit rumpled due to how it hung off Jenny's shoulder where the strap of her backpack pulled against it.

Meg could not see her own black hair, which hung loosely around her shoulders, but she imagined it moving as wildly as Jenny's did, as wild as her ragged breathing and the redness in her blue eyes. Jenny's face was pale and blotchy from fatigue, and she looked exhausted, but she had something about her. It was the determined set of her jaw or the set expression of resolve that hung upon her face like an avatar of hope. Meg could not tell if Jenny was telling the truth or not—if only because she did not know how to look for honesty—but she felt sure that Jenny spoke to it regardless of if it was true or not.

They crossed the parking lot together and entered through the doors of the school building, moving down a long corridor decorated with inspirational posters of dolphins, earth, and people sharing. At the end of the corridor was a bulletin board with an advertisement for the upcoming field day. They stopped at a door with a window of transparent plastic and glass. Inside were two young women, their old classmates Tish and Leanne, sharing their morning recess. They opened the glass door, entered through it, and stood aside as two excited youthful voices rang out as one.

Both girls smiled when they saw Meg and Jenny walking in.

"Hey guys," Leanne said brightly. "What's up?"

"Hey," Tish announced. "Whatcha doing today?"

Tish was a short girl who loved sports, and she walked with an extremely easy gait. She was always smiling, with her happiness reflected in her voice. Her blonde hair was straight and thick, hanging loosely down to the middle of her back. She had bright green eyes and dark, full lips, and her hair was pulled back to expose her neck. She stood with her hands clasped in front of her and looked like she was walking in place.

"Really nothing much," Jenny said.

"So, super lame?" Tish asked.

"I had something to do."

"And what's that?" Tish asked.

Jenny blushed. "I have to go to the bathroom."

Meg's eyes widened, and she laughed.

"No, really," Jenny said, lowering her voice. "I really do."

"Right," said Tish. She led them to the girls' bathroom and walked in with Jenny. Meg wandered over to a vending machine and started digging in her pocket for change.

Through the window, they could see a man leaning against a tree at the other end of the sidewalk, watching the school and smoking a cigarette. His eyes were cold and empty. He reminded Meg of her father, only skinnier.

"I've been busy. I'm a little behind on some things." Jenny said.

"Like what?" Tish asked.

"I'm working on an essay. I don't want to be here right now."

"Did you miss the essay topic?" Tish asked, with sarcasm in her voice.

Jenny turned on the faucet and began washing her hands.

"I don't have to give you the answer to that," Jenny said.

"Don't you have to hand it in or something?"

Jenny raised her voice. "I'm not telling you anything."

"It's too bad you weren't paying attention to the essay topic. You would have known not to choose one like that."

"Excuse me? What is it to you?" she asked, storming out of the restroom.

Tish followed her out. "Are you serious?"

"Tish," Meg said, "Can you lay off Jenny a bit? Stop being a pushy dick."

"Are you going to tell us?" Leanne joined in.

Jenny headed toward their recess class, ignoring the others. Meg and the others followed her in and took their seats. The teacher was a substitute and did not seem to want to even be there. His face was staring into a book as the class came in.

Leanne leaned over. "I know very well you heard me. Are you going to tell us about what you've been doing all weekend? Because we don't know. We didn't know you were dating. We didn't know you had a life. Are you going to tell us what's going on?"

Meg laughed and tilted her head, shifting her gaze to the ceiling. "We are just intrigued. We want to hear about your plans, your dreams and aspirations, and your love life."

Jenny shrugged. Her voice was thin, a treble-stringed instrument. "I can't tell you anything," she said. "It's all confidential."

Meg crinkled her nose. "It's confidential. Right. You can't tell us. Whatever."

"That's right." The two sat in silence for a minute before Jenny spoke again. "It's a secret," she reiterated.

"You're kidding me," Tish said.

The two girls looked at each other, then glanced away. They didn't want to get into an argument. Instead, they smiled at the questions they could answer.

"I'll bet you want a cigarette," Tish said.

"I'm quitting," Jenny answered. "I need to quit because I don't have enough money for cigarettes."

"You're quitting your life," Tish said. " No more cigarettes, no more parties, no more fun. You're just using up your time."

"What are you talking about?" Jenny asked.

"You have to have something to do. If you do nothing, you'll get bored."

"I am bored," Jenny said. "I'm bored with this."

"I mean, what's left for you? Where are you going with your life?" Leanne asked.

"I'm bored with all of that stuff," Jenny said. "I'm bored with feeling like shit all the time."

Tish leaned in. "You're bored with your social life. You're bored with the way your life is going, and you're bored of the way your life is going to be."

"Are you going to tell us about your life?" Meg continued.

Jenny said firmly, "I will tell no one anything."

"Why not?" Meg asked.

Jenny whipped around and spoke. "I will not tell you anything about anything because it's all my business."

Jenny bit her lip and closed her eyes, trying to hold back the tears to no avail. They were enormous and white; they rolled down her cheeks like beautiful pearls.

The surrounding others were used to this act now. She was a familiar face; one they were used to seeing but not really listening to.

They were all waiting for the bell to ring, waiting for the break to end, waiting for the next class to start. Mostly, they just put their heads down and closed their eyes, relying on their phones to keep them entertained until the bell rang. Some people put their phones away, but most of them still checked for texts or TikTok posts, or notifications from their favorite apps.

THREE

The Sheriff sat on the couch in his house by himself. A warm plate of macaroni and cheese sat atop his coffee table, but he was too distracted to eat it. Leo, his German Shepherd mix, lazed on the floor beside him. The house was quiet save for the TV, the only sound breaking the eerie silence of an empty house. The big screen flickered with an image of a burning building.

He found himself unable to wrap his mind around the murder. How could there have been no trace of blood?

What would he have done if he had committed this crime?

He realized he would have had to clean the body. A bathtub would have been too obvious, so he would have had to scrub the blood off and then dump it in the trash or off a bridge or into a river or lake. The murderer had to be someone who had access to a vehicle, which meant that he could have driven out on some country road and dumped it there.

Finally taking a bite of his macaroni, he chewed it slowly. There were no suspects. There were no leads for him to follow. He had interrogated people, and they had given him nothing; he had interrogated people, and they had given him something, but it wasn't good enough. His stomach growled. He added a bit of pepper to his macaroni to spice things up and took another bite.

The press that hounded him daily had already caught wind of the murder after the events that took place at the mines, and they were hungry for a story. So far, Madison had been holding off the leaders of the press and the prying eyes for him, and he was grateful for it.

The Sheriff chewed and swallowed, but something was not quite right. He stared at his plate of food and realized that he didn't even feel like eating. Losing his appetite, he rose and strode to the kitchen to get something to take his mind off the murder. Taking a bottle of vodka out of the freezer, he poured himself a glass. He knew he should not drink again, but he couldn't help himself. He tipped the glass and took a swig. There was a pack of cigarettes inside the drawer. He lit one.

Sitting back down on the couch, he put his arm around Leo. Leo tilted his head to the side, his eyes popping open wider, catching on to the movement. He wagged his tail silently, waiting for him to say something more. The Sheriff smiled at him.

"I don't know what's going on," he said. "I don't know who did it."

Leo licked his paw.

"There are no real good leads, and no one knows what happened, Leo."

Leo is a good listener, he thought. Hardly ever making a sound, the dog just sat there and looked at him.

"This is probably the worst murder we've ever had. No one is safe. No one is ever safe when there's a killer on the loose."

He didn't want to think about it anymore, so with a sigh, he picked up his plate of macaroni and headed into the kitchen, dumping it into the trash can and then scrubbing the plate lazily with a sponge.

He put his plate back on the table and poured himself another glass of vodka, lit another cigarette, and sat back down on the couch. He turned the TV back on and watched the news for a few minutes.

He sighed. He had to get out of the house. Turning off the TV with its steady talking heads (the news was always bad, always about more problems, more destruction, more riots, and murders) he went over to his dresser. He took out his gun. It was still in the holster. He unstrapped it and flipped open the safety compartment, checking to make sure it was loaded, and then snapped the strap back into place. He secured it around his waist and put on his coat. Last night, he had polished his boots and left them by the front door so he wouldn't forget them. Tonight, he might need them. This would not be good.

He picked up his car keys for a moment before putting them back down on the counter. He glanced at his liquor cabinet, reached over, and grabbed another bottle of vodka. This would help him relax as well as steady his hand if he had to use the gun tonight.

He snapped off the TV as he left the house. The sudden silence was deafening. He shook his head at the sensation of a rock band playing inside his skull and set off down the path to the street, locking the door behind him.

Sliding behind the wheel, he turned the key in the ignition. The engine turned over, and the car purred to life. Sliding into reverse, he backed out of the driveway.

The street was empty. It was cold out, and almost everyone was inside. Pulling out onto the street, he gunned the engine, speeding down the road. He was not in the mood to drive slowly. Instead, he wanted to get to his destination even quicker so he could get this over with.

He drove until he reached downtown, navigating until he found the right road. The road came to a dead-end after he turned onto it. He parked and got out of the car making sure he locked it and walked up to the house. Pausing for a moment he looked through the window at the woman who lived there.

Lucinda Johnson was an 81-year-old widow who lived alone. As if her legs were too heavy for her to support, she was clean, careful, and hobbled when she walked. She could also be hard of hearing, especially when there was a lot of ambient noise. She lived in a small town in which everyone knew everyone, but she was not well-liked. Some called her snooty; others said she was fickle and possessive about her sons because of their father's premature death. She kept to herself, living in a small house with few windows that faced away from one another. She had volunteered at school plays and bazaars that no one else had heard about. Her house was in eye and earshot of where the body was found.

Going up to the door, the sheriff banged on it with his fist. He waited for a few beats of silence and banged again. "Mrs. Johnson?" He waited for a reply but didn't hear one. He thought had perhaps gone to visit someone else and wasn't home. About to give up, he heard the door open. He turned around, and after a series of creaks and pops, the door slowly opened.

She stood in the doorway, arms crossed and glaring at him. Her rheumy eyes watched his wide shoulders and tall frame. She looked him up and down without blinking.

"What do you want?" she asked bluntly.

"Just a few questions," the Sheriff said.

"Already gave a statement."

"I know," he said with a wry smile, "but this is just proce-dure."

"I don't see why you need to do this," she said, stabbing her cane into the floor. "I'm not going anywhere."

"No," he said with a bow from his waist, "no, you're not."

"Why are you bowing?" she asked. "It's awkward."

The Sheriff didn't move.

"Alright," she said. "You've made your point. Come in."

Entering the house, he could see that it was dark and cluttered. The cupboards in the kitchen were full and there were pictures of family on the walls. The Sheriff wanted to do this questioning as quickly as possible. He was more interested in justice than in understanding.

"So," she said. "What is the nature of this questioning?"

"First," he said. "Do you have anything to drink?"

"What?" The old woman looked at him with a confused expression.

"Didn't you hear me?" he asked. "It's not a crime to ask for a drink."

Her eyes bored into his for a long moment. He could see the confusion on her face.

"Yes, it is."

"No, it isn't."

Her face grew stern, and she looked at him through narrowed eyes.

"Yes, it is."

"No, it isn't," he stated, his tone offering a sense of finality.

"Alright," she mumbled. "I'll make some coffee."

As she went into the kitchen, he watched her. The coffee pot, the water pitcher, the filters, and the mugs were all gathered by her. Pouring the water into the coffee machine, she then set a mug down on the counter. She poured the water into the mug, and after a few minutes, appeared again. She brought the mug with her and handed it to the sheriff. He took it and drank it. It wasn't the best cup of coffee he had ever had, but it was hot, and he was thirsty.

"So," he began. "I just want to ask a few questions about the incident."

"Okay," she said. "What do you want to know?"

"How did you hear the screams?" The Sheriff asked.

"What?" she asked.

"How did you know you heard screams?" he asked.

"Because I heard them."

"No, I mean, how did you know the screaming was screaming? Could it have been something else?"

"I knew they were screams because I heard them."

"Alright. Did you hear anything at all? Anything at all before the screaming occurred?"

"I don't understand."

"Did you hear anything before the screaming, anything unusual?"

"No."

He breathed in the scent of his cup of coffee. The dark, rich aroma calmed him and took his mind off the stress of this case. Except it wasn't working. The scent of the coffee wasn't helping him find a solution any faster. He had some ideas, but he knew that at this point the ideas were just little sparks that needed more time to catch fire and ignite.

"Alright," he said. "Let's start over. How did you know they were screams?"

"Because I heard them."

"Yes, I know that. I want you to use your own words."

"I heard the screams because they were loud, and they were shrill."

"I see," the Sheriff said. "What did you do when you heard them?"

"I called the police."

"Right," the Sheriff said. "Who did you call?"

"The police."

"No, I mean, who did you call? The Sheriff's office?"

"Yes."

"Good," The Sheriff said. "Tell me, did you notice any-thing unusual beforehand?"

"No."

"Did you notice anything unusual during?" he asked again, gentler, his voice almost a whisper.

She took a shuddering breath. "No."

"Did you notice anything unusual after?"

She furrowed her brow and shook her head. "No," she said.

"No?" He asked.

She looked at him with a confused expression. She said nothing. For a while, she stared at him. He watched her, patiently. She looked as if she was considering speaking, but she was uncertain about what to say.

"Okay," the Sheriff noted after a few moments of silence. He stood up, feeling as though any more questions wouldn't get him any further. He was going to finish recording this statement and then he was going to forget about it.

"Thank you for your time, Mrs. Johnson. I can help myself out."

Turning, he walked towards the door. Hearing footsteps behind him, he turned around to see her walking quickly behind him. He stopped, and she walked up to him, stopping just before she collided with him. She was panting a little, and her face was red. Her walker was a few feet away, and she had walked almost the entire length of her house to reach him.

"Is there something wrong?" he asked.

"Okay," she said. "I didn't hear the screams... I saw something."

The Sheriff furrowed his brow. "What do you mean?"

"I saw eyes," she said. "I saw red eyes glowing in the window."

"I don't understand."

"I saw them in my window. They were watching me. The eyes."

Her eyes darted down and then back up, an almost imperceptible movement. The Sheriff furrowed his brow.

"That," she said. "That is what I saw." With her index finger, she pointed at him. She pressed it against his forearm, then shook her head. Sighing, she returned to her chair.

Frowning, he asked, "What?"

"I saw them watching me," she said. "I saw them looking in the window."

"What are you talking about?" he asked. He was wondering about the state of her mental health.

"They looked like eyes, but they weren't not normal," she said.

Her voice cracked as she spoke, and tears streamed silently down her face. "They were more like a wild animal's." She paused for a moment and took a deep breath. He was almost certain that she couldn't see him. Her eyes were open, but she was not alert. She was absent. It was as if her mind was somewhere else. She had her mouth hanging open, either slack-jawed or about to speak. He could see the muscles in her neck tighten as she pulled in a deep breath of warm air.

"They had red eyes," she said. "They were watching me."

She pointed at him, and the Sheriff flinched. He took a step back and then another. He was finding it hard to breathe. Her eyes were wide, and her mouth was open, and he could see her tongue and her teeth. She was staring forward, unblinking. She was speaking, but he was certain that she didn't know what she was saying. And then she pointed again, and a chill ran down his spine.

"They were watching me," she said again, and her eyes flicked upwards. The Sheriff looked up and saw nothing but the ceiling, beige and bland and pale, identical to every other ceiling in every other house in every other development in the world.

"What are you talking about?"

"I saw them," she said. "I saw the eyes of monsters." She pointed at him again. "I saw them watching me."

The Sheriff took another step back. His left foot bumped into something, and he looked down. It was her walker. He looked back up at her. She was still looking at him, her eyes vacant but her lips moving.

"I'm sorry, I have to go."

"Wait," she said.

She reached out a hand and grabbed his arm. She looked at her withered hand on his arm. Her eyes filled with unshed tears as she looked over his firm muscles and young skin, up to his face. He looked down at her tear-filled eyes. He looked around at her wild, white hair and flushed, red face and the hands that he knew were old, but which still held his arm so firmly. She opened her mouth to speak, slowly shook her head and sighed, then opened her mouth again. Her lips moved as she formed the words and spoke to him softly, silently. Her brow creased, her eyes glistened, and she smiled.

"My cats," she said. "I need to feed my cats."

Her hand fell from his arm, and she returned to her chair. She watched him go, not knowing what else to do. He paused at the backdoor and turned around. He looked at her for a moment and then walked out. She was alone once again. The Sheriff stood there for a moment, more confused than when he had walked into the house, and then strode away, down the driveway and back to his car.

FOUR

M adison could not fall asleep. Her head was buzzing with thoughts and questions about the murder. She didn't want to wake up her boyfriend, so she was sitting silently at the kitchen table in her pajamas. The air was thick with the smell of coffee and a faint smell of garbage from the alley behind her apartment building. A ceiling fan stirred the stale air but brought no relief from the stink. Two cockroaches ran along the edges of the table, waving their antennae at passing crumbs. The fat insects were so out of place in Madison's orderly apartment that they seemed like intruders or bizarre hallucinations. If she tried to kill them now, they would multiply, like so many children running around a house on Christmas morning. The horrid thought made Madison shudder, and she moved to a different seat at the kitchen table, trying to shake off the thought.

Madison had always been this way—a worrier who felt uneasy whenever there were people or things that did not fit into their proper places. She could not stand for things to be out of order, especially not in her own home. It made her feel like everything might fall apart around her at any moment like she had no control over anything or anyone in her life. This feeling made Madison sad and angry at herself for not being able to get things under control.

It was late at night, and she had not slept a wink. She had sat there for hours studying the case notes. She looked at them every night and still; she had nothing to go on.

Sipping her coffee, she found herself unable to even take a bite of her muffin. She waved a fly away from her face and watched as it fluttered over to the window. She looked at the window and then back at her muffin.

She felt like she was at the end of her rope, her apartment was too small, her neighbors were assholes, her boss was an idiot sometimes, and they would never solve the case they were working on.

She looked at her muffin and finally bit into it. The fresh, warm taste of blueberries and butter filled her mouth and her stomach. Taking a sip of her coffee, she felt the hot liquid burn her lips. She took another sip and then another. She finished the cup, and she felt a warm, tingling sensation spread out from her toes, up through her legs, and into her hips. Her eyelids drooped shut, and she tried to shake the fuzziness out of her head. She felt as if she were afloat on a gentle wave. Just as she was about to nod off, she leaned her head back and noticed something outside of the window.

The window was full of cobwebs, but she could clearly see the alley through them. A figure was standing and facing her window. She saw it stand there for a moment before walking around the side of the building. She watched the figure saunter over to a lamppost and stop. It covered its slender body in simple robes; the hood pulled up over its head. She couldn't make out its facial features.

Her heart pounded in her chest, and she leaned down to turn off the light in the kitchen. She might have made a sound, but if so, it was not enough for them to hear. Now, she could watch them without alerting them to her presence. Though the shadow cast by the moon made it difficult to see, she could make out their shape in front of the window and could tell from their demeanor that they were huge.

A row of trees blocked her view of the house's entrance, but she could see the figure at the door continue to stand and stare in her direction. It almost seemed as if their eyes glowed red.

Her service revolver was in the bedroom and right now, that seemed a thousand miles away. Crickets chirped high in the trees, and she shivered.

The figure glided slowly and casually, but with a purpose. It knew where it was going.

She saw it look up and point a finger at her, then put the finger to its lips, as if to shush her. Even from a distance, she could see the knob of knuckles rise off the skin before it dove back into the sunless depths. The person knew she was in the room. It knew that she was watching from behind the glass, and yet it continued to come closer to her apartment wall.

She turned the light on and looked at the window. It stopped and tilted its head, staring into her soul. Suddenly, she heard a thud—her boyfriend fell off the bed and hit the floor.

"What the hell?" she exclaimed.

Her boyfriend jumped up and walked out of the bedroom and into the kitchen, looking around for her. She sat frozen in her chair, eyes wide, her heart beating rapidly in her chest.

Her boyfriend cocked an eyebrow and stared, looking at her like she had sprouted a second head.

"What's wrong?" he asked.

"I saw someone outside."

"What?"

She walked toward him. "I don't know what, but I saw them."

"You ok? You seem terrified." He asked.

She felt his hand on her bare shoulder, which was goose-pimpled in the chilly night air. Her skin was cold, clammy, and hard, like the feeling someone gets when they must tell a friend that their mother just passed away.

"Any idea who it was?" he asked.

"I don't know. I didn't get a good look at them. They looked up and saw me. They pointed at me and then put a finger to their lips," she said, looking into his eyes, full of fear.

The way she was acting had him puzzled and concerned.

"Well, let me think," he said.

Her boyfriend was normally slow to act, and even slower when he was tired. With each blink, his eyelids fell lower, as if weighed down by lead. Rubbing his eyes, he peered at his watch.

"You didn't see what they looked like?" he asked.

"No, I couldn't get a good look at them. I saw a robe, a hood."

"So, they were a person?"

"Yes, obviously, you fucking dumbass."

"So, I don't know. Maybe it was the same drunk guy? I wouldn't worry about it."

Her boyfriend walked to the door and double-checked the locks. He walked back to the kitchen and looked at her.

"I'm tired, babe, and I'm going back to bed. You should get some sleep. You've been working too hard."

He left the kitchen and walked down the hall to their bedroom, but she didn't turn back to watch him go. A breeze lifted the thin white curtains and stirred them like wisps of smoke. She could see the parking lot below, but no one was there now. She heard her boyfriend snoring and then crawled into bed with a sigh. When she closed her eyes, she felt safe from whatever might be outside the window. She dreamed of a black figure standing in the kitchen doorway, in a long, thin robe that swayed about his knees, with a dark and muffled mask over its face. It had blood dripping off its knife-hand, raising the knife high above its head and then wobbling it down toward her face. Then it pointed at its lips.

"Shhhhh," it whispered.

FIVE

I t was a warm night, with light rain falling. The wipers moved back and forth with a soft slssshhh. The sheriff drove his cruiser to the station. He was going over his case notes and thinking about the murder. The more he thought about it, the more he knew he was right. The killer was probably from out of town. There was no way that someone from this town would do this. He did not know why he thought that, but it made the most sense. Everything pointed to it. Two victims weren't robbed, and the murder weapon was a sharp blade. A big knife.

His brakes screeched, and it threw the car in front of him to the side. Sparks flew from its undercarriage, and it careened straight toward the ditch. A red car rushed up and t-boned its side. Metal crunched and glass shattered. In his rearview, he saw the red car speed away. The car in front of him veered to the side at a high rate of speed, narrowly missing the ditch. He looked in his rearview and saw the red car close in on him. The sound of squealing tires filled the surrounding air, but he remained still, frozen by the sudden violence revealed to him. He slammed on his brakes, but it was too late. The car was coming fast behind him and was moving too quickly to be stopped by a simple maneuver. He turned the wheel and spun off onto the shoulder of the road. The car closed in on him and then he lost sight of it. His heart pounded fast inside his chest, thinking that the sound of crashing metal would tear through the air at any moment, but it never came.

He tried to wheeze and cough, but it got caught in his chest. Feeling like he would smother he remembered his flask. He pulled it out and took a long sip. The cold liquid burned his throat as it slid down into his stomach, but it did not help allay the heat he felt in his chest. He reached out and opened the driver's side window. The cool air of the outside swirled in, catching the red light of his brake lights. He looked at them but did not put on his lights. The car was half a mile behind him. He could not worry about them now. There were bigger things to worry about.

He put his flask away and then drove to the station. Seeing what time it was he put on his lights and sped up, though the road was empty. He drove fast and then pulled into the station parking lot. The lot was half full, though most of the cars were police vehicles. He parked and walked into the building, plodding over to the conference room. He opened the door and looked at everyone sitting at the table, poring over two large binders.

"I'm sorry I'm late," he denoted.

"No problem, everyone was here before you," said Derrick. Derrick was his part-time deputy who also worked as a teacher at the high school.

Madison took a deep breath and let it out slowly. She closed her eyes, but her hands never rested. Writing something on a legal pad, she looked up. Her eyes still had not opened all the way. She smiled at him, with tired eyes. She had her hair tied back, and her glasses sat firmly on her nose.

"You look tired," he said.

"I am. I had a rough night," she replied.

"Anything you want to talk about?"

"No, I'll be fine."

"All right,"

They took inventory of the details, chased leads, and probed for holes in their logic. Going over the reports from the coroner and the lab, they took a bigger picture view of the case, trying to piece together all the details and make sense of it. They had a thread to follow, but it led back to a void.

"So, do we have anything?" the sheriff asked.

"No, nothing really," said Derrick.

Madison shook her head. "How about the victims? Is there anything odd about them?"

"No connections to anything or each other," Derrick sighed.

"What about the crime scenes?" Madison asked.

"There were two small drops of blood on the clothing of the victim and a few strands of blonde hair, around six inches long. Other than that, there's nothing," Madison mumbled in response to herself.

"Anything on the clothing?" the sheriff asked.

"No, we got nothing from the clothing. The blood was from the victims, but there was no DNA from the killer," she said.

"Ok, so maybe the killer is a drifter. Someone who was passing through town," said the sheriff.

The light in her eyes grew dim for a moment, then she shook it off.

"So, we have a drifter who is killing people," said Derrick.

"Or he is targeting the town." The sheriff said.

"Why would anyone target this town?" she asked.

Shaking his head, the sheriff replied, "I wish I knew. Maybe he has a personal vendetta against the people of Pine Creek. Maybe he has a family member that was on the losing side of things. There are too many possibilities, and we don't have enough to go off."

The sheriff stood up and stretched his back. "I spoke to Lucinda again. She just went on about glowing eyes. I don't think she'll be much of a witness, I'm afraid."

"So, we have no actual witnesses, no DNA, no murder weapon, no nothing?" asked Madison.

"No, we have a killer. He has already killed two people and he'll definitely try to kill again. We need to find him before he succeeds," he answered.

The sheriff walked out of the room, went back to his office, and sat down in his chair, sighing. Closing his eyes, he thought about the case, going over it in his mind and trying to think of something they might have missed. He knew they were missing something, but what? He opened his eyes and looked at the door. Outside was a cool morning. He heard birds chirping and saw the sun peeking in through the window.

Opening the top drawer of his desk, he pulled out a large brown envelope. He opened it and looked at the pictures of the crime scenes inside. The photographs showed the dead girl from the first murder, a cigarette still dangling from her fingers. Part of her left breast had been torn away, revealing a network of vessels, fat, and muscle that had been stripped bare of life and blood. He studied the photographs and then looked at the coroner's report. Its cold detachment made the crime scene photographs seem cozy by comparison. Both victims were drained completely of blood and their organs removed in ways that suggested a ritual. Though the cause of death was listed as exsanguination or blood loss, he wondered if that was really what had happened. Both victims also had strange carvings on their chests.

He took a sip of his coffee and let its hot flavor roll over his tongue. He held the bitter, hot liquid in his mouth for a moment and then swallowed. The contented grin on his face told stories of years spent re-discovering what he knew to be great pleasures in the face of a world that often denied him even small moments of happiness.

He flipped through the pages of the autopsy report. The smell of stale coffee and old paper filled the surrounding air. He took another sip of coffee as he turned through the stack of papers until he found what he was looking for: a list of things that had been taken from the body. He looked at it for a moment and then ran through it in his head, mentally adding up the numbers.

Then he went to another stack of files on his desk, one that he did not leave out when civilians visited him at work because of its unsavory contents, namely unsolved murder cases with information gaps. He pulled out all the files that matched the list he had just seen on the coroner's report. Each murder had taken place recently, but both appeared as though they belonged to some dark age in human history where murder was commonplace. How many more victims were there? Was there some kind of Jack the Ripper serial killer loose in Pine Creek? A chill ran down his spine at the thought.

His mind was blank as he tried to remember any unexplained murders. He wanted to think that he had been wrong about the pattern and that this was just an isolated incident, but every instinct told him otherwise. So, he tried to think of the previous years. He thought of the young girl who had been found covered in blood on the side of the road. The town still talked about her, and no one knew if it was an intentional murder or a cover-up for an accident. There were never any suspects put forward, though, and nothing ever came of it.

He sat and wondered about the notes he had seen at the crime scenes. They had writing on each finger. He did not believe that they were going to help the killer. He thought they were rituals or something. But what was the purpose?

He walked into the hallway and then into the bathroom. He splashed cold water on his face and looked at himself in the mirror. "What am I missing?" he asked.

His brown eyes stared back at him. The small lines around his nose and the gray hairs in his beard stared back at him, too. When he smiled, he saw the wrinkles forming around his eyes and at the corners of his mouth. He could see the sun lines on his face, the ones from the days when he would go to the beach and swim in shiny waves. The rough skin of a life lived hard and fast, covered his features. Living through months and years of challenging work filled his days of nothing but putting one foot in front of the other. He wondered how much time had passed, but he knew it didn't matter how long it took to solve this case; he was going to solve it. After staring at himself in the mirror for a long time, he finally walked out of the bathroom.

SIX

G rant Harbridge walked through the woods to the little cottage that had been his home for the last few months. He kept to himself and living off the land was something he had been doing for a very long time. He had gone to town twice to pick up some supplies, but he never stayed long.

The people gave him a lot of strange looks, and he wasn't accustomed to that kind of attention. After the sun had set, he preferred the solitude of the woods and the quiet of the forest. His long arms were swinging from side to side as he walked through the trees. His feet crunched against the dry ground as he walked with a long, heavy stride. He wore a red flannel shirt and dark blue jeans. He had on old boots, and a bandana was wrapped around his face and tied behind his head. Pushing the brush aside, he stepped into the small clearing in front of his house. He walked up to the front door. It was a small wooden building with a slanted roof that came to a point at the top. He reached up and grabbed the doorknob. As he pulled the door open, he looked around the house. He had been learning how to make furniture in the few weeks he had been in the town, but he was still getting the hang of working with wood.

Some of his pieces were better than others, but most of them were decent. He had made a bed, a couple of tables, and a few chairs. There was a small fireplace, and a locked cabinet to keep his valuables in. He went inside and closed the door behind him. He walked to the fireplace and threw a small bird onto the fire. There was a loud crackling sound as the flames spread out and enveloped the pile of sand and sticks, he had put there. He sat back and watched the fire burn, entranced by the way the flames danced.

Having walked for several hours, he was thirsty. He stood up and walked to the cabinet next to the fireplace, opened it up, and pulled out a bottle of clear liquid. He pulled the top off the bottle and took a swig of the liquor and then put the bottle back into the cabinet and closed it.

He walked to the bedroom and sat down on the bed. Pulling his flannel shirt up over his head, he threw it on the floor. He ran his hands through his hair and leaned back against the wooden headboard. He was a tall, muscular man. His dark hair was long and fell around his shoulders. It was usually matted and messy from days of not being washed or brushed. He pulled his pants down to his ankles and rested his head on the bed. He sighed and took another drink.

"Now that is more like it," he mumbled, his words slurred.

The harsh fumes bit at his throat and chest. Just a few gulps went a long way, even though it smelled funny and tasted even worse. The fire felt like raindrops on his skin. An orgasmic rush filled him from head to toe, spreading down from his brain towards his toes, as images of running through fields with trees around him came to life. His arms stretched out wide, welcoming the imaginary world in with open arms.

He had only been there for a few weeks when he had first started feeling that he should leave. He tried to ignore it, but he kept feeling like someone was watching him. Then he heard voices in his head. Well, it wasn't as much of an audible voice as it was a voice that he felt. It wasn't a terrible voice, though. It was a wonderful voice, and it was a voice that he liked to listen to. He was told to go deeper into the woods. The voice told him to build a house and live off the land. It told him to forget about all the people that were in town. He had obeyed the voice and started building his house.

He liked the quietness of the woods. He liked the way his muscles felt when he worked in his house. His body had not felt this good in a long time. After his wife died, he stopped working out. He had been in the woods for a long time. He had gotten to a point where he did not know what was real anymore.

He got to a point where he didn't know what he was doing or why.

He was hazily awake but did not know why. The voice told him to get up. Standing in front of the mirror, naked and dripping sweat, he looked at his body. He looked thinner than he ever had before, and his muscle mass was gone. His body was boney, and it didn't even look human.

He looked down at the ground that was covered in wood chips and the dust from inside the house. He was looking for something, and he didn't know what it was.

"What the hell are you looking for?" the voice in his head asked.

"I don't know," he replied.

"Well, why don't you go out and get it?" the voice continued.

His heart was beating. His stomach dropped, and an uneasy feeling filled his stomach. He wanted to sleep again. He wanted to go back to being unconscious. Maybe it was better that way because he had his doubts. He wasn't sure whether he was a man or a bear. He wasn't sure what he was supposed to do. The burning between his legs was too strong to think about that anymore. Too weak to do anything he needed to sleep. He needed to sleep a lot. Walking over to his bed, he laid down.

His stomach growled. He was still hungry. His stomach was never quiet, but now it was louder than ever. He heard a loud noise coming from his ribcage. It felt like a ball of fire was trapped inside him burning his stomach from the inside out. He was hungry. It had been several days since he had eaten anything substantial. His food supply was running dangerously low. Standing up, he grabbed a box of dry oats and took it outside. He sat down on the porch and ate every bit of food, thinking that he would have to hunt for more.

Looking around, he was confused. He hadn't spoken to anyone, and no one had talked to him for a while now either. It felt like his throat was dry and full of sand, and it was hard to breathe. He looked at the ground. There was a dead bird there. It looked like a robin. It had died of natural causes; he was sure. He picked up the bird and held it in his hand. The sour smell of death infiltrated his nostrils. He was disgusted, but he still put the bird into his mouth with little hesitation. There was a large, crunching sound as the bird was crushed between his teeth.

He was hungry, even though it tasted horrible. It felt like there was a lump in his throat. It felt like something had risen from his stomach and made it to his mouth and now it was stuck there, choking him. His heartbeat was loud, and it was audible over the sound of the rest of the woods. It almost sounded like thunder. It was his heart thumping against his chest that made the sound. The taste of the bird was nauseating.

An enormous sound then pierced through the trees. The sound was like a waterfall crashing into rocks, but it was softer. Then there was a loud splash that echoed off the leaves and the long stems of the ferns. It was a sound like a giant wave crashing into the shore. At first, he thought it was thunder. It sounded like thunder, but it had stopped raining and there were no clouds in the sky. His breath caught in his throat, and he could feel his heart pounding inside his chest.

"I am here," the voice said.

He scanned the horizon and the tree line stretching out before him. His eyes cut through the darkening blue of the sky until they rested upon a small shape moving quickly towards him. It was too far away to discern details, but he knew it was heading towards him. He stood frozen as he watched it weave craftily in and out of the trees. He ran towards the noise just as the voice had told him to. He ran as fast as he could through the woods until he broke through the tree line onto a high grassy hill. The closer he got to the sound, the more he recognized it. He remembered hearing it before, in his mind all those weeks ago, when she had told him to come here. It was her voice.

Her voice was beautiful. The melody was not music. It was like a distant, high-pitched tone, a pitch that was almost painful when heard. It was pulling him back, pushing him away from here. The closer he got, the stronger the sensation became, until the world around him felt like it was spinning without moving. There was a terror gripping him harshly and a pain ringing in his head, and it was pushing him back away from her. His feet stopped running before he got to her, but he didn't know why they stopped running.

There was something reaching for him, something drawing him to it. The smell of flower petals filled his head like smoke, and all he could think about was falling into them, being lost forever in their world of reds and purples and blues, of perfumes and alien smells and pollen dusting his skin.

He felt like there was a scream in the world, screaming into his ears and searing his skin, alerting the hidden parts of him that crouched in the darkness of his soul like wolves beside their den.

He felt like there was an anger in the world, a wave of anger that robbed him of his strength and filled him with fire. He felt like there were pieces missing from him as if he had fallen through a hole and could not find an edge to climb back out of, as if there were pieces missing from him, he would never find again. He felt like there were things he should do, things he should not do, things he should say to her and things he should not say to her and the things he should explain to her, and things he should never try to explain to anyone in the entire world. It made no sense to anyone who did not know what they had seen each other do or what they had done together alone, but it made perfect sense to him because she made sense to him.

"Come to me," the voice said. A twig snapped behind him. Terrified, he could hear footsteps approaching him. Paralyzed, he couldn't even breathe. The footsteps were getting closer and closer.

He could hear her heart beating, and his own heart skipped a beat in anticipation. She was right behind him, and he could smell her perfume. He could smell the scent of her body. He could smell her skin. Her blood flowed through her veins to pump her heart, and he could hear it in his ears and feel it in his belly and taste it in his mouth. His blood pumped through his veins and drummed in his ears and swelled in his jaw as if his flesh were about to burst with the pressure. He felt her breath against his neck, as sweet and warm as honey, sliding down the back of his throat. She breathed into him, filling him with air, filling him with life.

Standing tall and proud, he turned around to face her. In her eyes, he could see all the love in the world. He could feel it beating in his chest, rising from his knees, and flowing down into his toes. He loved her. She was perfection. She was everything he had ever wanted and was everything he had ever needed.

"I'm here," she spoke, in a voice that rang like a bell, deep and pure and beautiful.

Her words were simple, easy to understand, and yet they sounded like an ocean crashing against rocks, like birds singing at sunrise, like waves tumbling to shore. Inside his chest, he felt them as though they were his own heart-beat—deep and pure and beautiful. Her long legs hung quietly in the frozen air. Her pale skin shone like ivory satin in the gentle light of the moon, which cut through the cool night air and played over her body like a lover's caress. She was beauty incarnate. She was a goddess.

She grabbed him and threw him to the ground. Pressing her weight down onto him, she trapped him beneath her. Her arms wrapped around his back. She could feel his muscles shift beneath her limbs as he struggled to escape. She was strong and a hungry strength burned inside her, fueled by a passion for life and a desire for what she wanted that frightened her as much as it freed her. The muscles in her arms were hard and held him like steel bands. His body writhed. But she did not move. She held him down. She felt something else, too—something soft and warm and pliant move beneath her skin as she held him, something that was tired of being held back by fear or doubt or worry or indecision. Pulling him into an embrace, he couldn't get her off him, no matter how hard he tried. They made her body for embracing and stroking, but there was nothing soft about what she did.

He didn't want to do anything. The knife was resting on the ground, inches from his fingers. It was a dull and smooth-edged instrument meant to cut and slice meat. It could cut more than that. He couldn't pick it up. He feared what he might do with it. His hands were shaking, and he couldn't steady them enough to lift the weapon. He didn't have to lift it far, just far enough to reach her neck. It was resting on the earth like a treasure, or a serpent, or a tool of justice. Prone on the ground before him, it seemed as harmless as any other object in the world.

He wanted to run away and hide in the fields, but he knew he was too weak for such a task. Deep down, he knew that he would have to get up eventually and make a choice, but for now, he could just lay there and pretend she had already made the choice for him. Stuck and lying on the ground, he didn't want to move. He lay there because he couldn't stand it anymore. The longer he lay there, the harder it was to get up.

He was nervous. She was standing over him with her hand raised high in the air, a look of pure hatred now in her eyes. The whites of her eyes became tinged with violet, and her irises bled away into the darkness of her pupils. He could almost hear the blood rushing through his ears and his breaths were shallow and quick. Her eyes burned into him like molten lava or embers from a wildfire deep in a forest at night—so red that it hurt him to look at them directly, and yet he could not look away. She stared at him like she was looking at her prey and he was terrified that she was right.

They stared at each other for what felt like centuries, as though time had stopped. Her hand trembled, and then it fell toward his head. Her fingers twitched, and then they were tumbling through the air. They seemed to float rather than fall. When they were just three inches away, they curled up toward the sky and back towards his head, making it seem like she had pushed him away. Her fingertips touched his scalp and slid along the contours of his skull. Something rushed through her at his skin's softness. He tried to pull her hand away, but it seemed to be glued to his head. The more he pulled, the more glued it became.

She grabbed his neck. Her hands were like iron, but her grip was not devastating. She was holding him close, and he could feel her hot breath on his lips. Next, she pushed him further into the ground, forcing him to lie on his back. She climbed atop him and straddled his body so there was no way he could move. He could feel the heat from her body, and he could smell her sweet perfume wafting from her hair. Her legs were sturdy, and there was no way for him to move them. His breathing quickened as he realized she had him pinned beneath her. Her eyes spoke of desire.

Holding his chin, she leaned in only to clamp her teeth over his throat. He felt then sink into his skin, and at that moment, he knew she would kill him. He grabbed her hand and pushed it away. Snatching at the air, she lunged for him again, and this time could hold on to his leg with both hands. Her eyes burned with a fiery light, and her face radiated with a red glow.

She took her two index fingers and used them to penetrate his mouth. She forced her fingers deep inside, past the lips, and deep into the mouth and throat. His scalp grew tight and hot with his rage and panic at the sensation of being completely controlled. His breath must have changed to choked gasps of horror because the creatures came up behind him and said, "He is mine."

He curled forward and the heat of the beasts pressed against his back like a furnace in a factory near his head. He breathed in their scent, which was pungent with a mix of sweat and pulverized flowers. The hands ran down his back and found his chest, which rose and fell beneath them.

Footsteps rumbled and scraped across the meadow, somewhere behind him, and then he heard a voice in his head that said "mine." Mine? They had been chasing him, he knew. It was his imagination, wasn't it? But it was getting closer. Closer. They were inches behind him, and he could hear the bellows of their breath in his ears behind him.

The smell of blood assaulted his senses, gagging him. It flowed in the air, clinging to his skin. It penetrated his clothing and clogged his nose and throat. He gasped for breath, struggling for oxygen. His chest heaved with effort.

The stinging smell burned the inside of his nose, throat, and lungs. He desperately tried to draw a breath, but each attempt ripped a coughing scream from his throat. His chest felt as though it were being crushed by a two-ton boulder. He could feel the oxygen leaving his body, and his heart raced. He was suffocating.

His jaw felt hot like it was on fire. He tried to open his mouth, but the woman had gripped his teeth with a vice-like pressure that went beyond pain. Feeling her fingers digging into the soft flesh of his cheeks and jaw, he couldn't open his mouth. He couldn't say anything only releasing muffled screams. A pressure on his chest grew steadily heavier as he felt himself being pushed down by a terrible, heavy, boulder-like weight. He was a statue, trapped under a heavy stone.

He struggled and thrashed his body as hard as he could. His teeth pressed into her hands. It took him several minutes to bite her fingers, but he did. There wasn't enough space in his throat to make a noise. His blood was flowing through his ears at a rapid rate. In the absence of oxygen, his muscles grew weak.

She held his hands away as she pulled her fingers from his mouth. He could feel his muscles contracting with every movement. He could smell her flesh and her blood, and he wanted neither more than he wanted the feel of her hands on his skin. Her flesh was pale and firm, like the talons of a falcon. Her hair fell over her shoulders in a black river and framed her face in a tangle of darkness that seemed to absorb all light. She grasped his wrists, pulling them up and pushing them down. He felt the sharp points of her teeth scraping against his skin.

She chewed on his skin, with cheek dimples and deep grooves from smiling. He felt her grinding her teeth into his skin, tearing at him. There was no biting or scratching. The thin layers of flesh were barely even a barrier between her and his blood. The other creatures were on all four legs, circling them, sniffing him. Then, the creature lifted its head and took a bite of his face. The thick, fleshy parts of him fell away with little more than a tug. Blood squirted through the air like a water pistol blasting out a constant stream. As if he were a wild turkey in a dance, they all started tearing at him. They were shouting and screaming. They ripped him to pieces. He heard their growls, and it felt as if someone had torn off both his arms. The pain was unbearable, and he screamed. He could feel it as they tore at his flesh.

Reaching down, she ripped his shirt open, revealing his chest. She tore his shirt from his body. He felt the fabric ripping and tearing away from his body, exposing his skin further.

A hand shot out and pulled a large knife from her dress, the flat of the blade cold and sparkling in the moonlight. Pressing the tip into the center of his chest, she sank deeply, drawing blood. He gasped. She carved the blade deep into his chest, his skin digging into the edge of the blade as she dug out another symbol and pressed it into his shoulder. She carved a deep gash into his shoulder, feeling the knobby ends of his bones press against the blade with each stroke. The skin on his arm and shoulder was sticky and slick. His breath hitched, and he cried out in pain with the little energy he had left.

She carved a symbol into his chest. He didn't know what the symbol meant, but it was beautiful.

Her hand was steady, driving the point of the knife deeper than he thought possible. He felt his ribs cracking, and he felt his internal organs splintering and breaking as she dug into him. A spurt of blood burst from his mouth, splashing onto her apron. He felt his head spinning and his vision was black. He felt like he was going to pass out. She paused, testing the weight of the knife in her hand, then lifted it into the air and brought it down again.

She removed the blade from his chest and held it right above where his heart was beating so quickly. She let the blade fall, and it sunk deep into his chest. It sliced into his flesh easily and slid between the bones of his rib cage, over the muscle and tissue of his heart, and through to the other side of his chest.

She could feel his heart racing faster as the blade sank into his chest. It pulsed against the blade as it came to life in her hands.

He could feel the blade pierce his heart. He could feel it sink into his chest. The cold metal pressed against the surface of his skin and pushed through, like a hot poker through a chunk of ice, like a needle through heavy leather. The muscle in his chest felt numb as it spasmed beneath her hand, jerking uncontrollably beneath her touch. He tried to breathe, but it felt unnatural like every breath sucked in more memories than air. The memories filled his lungs until he felt it cast each lung with a heavy lead that made each breath more effortful than the last. Each breath hurt, and he could feel them stabbing him in the back like knives twisting and ripping at the surface of his skin. Each breath caught in his throat like hot coals and burned at the back of his neck. He choked on the pain, and every breath made them burn harder as they ripped through his windpipe and tore at him from the inside out. Falling into darkness, his vision flickered and went completely black. He no longer knew where he was. His muscles collapsed, and he was empty inside.

Her eyes were wide and golden, and the wind was whipping her red cloak. the cloak bellowed out to either side of her like a loose sail over the prow of a ship.

The stiletto heels of her boots dug into the dirt beside his shoulder. She stood over the man she had raised to his knees before her, pulled up by the hands that had until recently rested comfortably on his shoulders. She tossed her long hair back out of her face, and it flowed down over the front of the cloak and over her chest, curling to rest below the neckline of her dress. Looking down at him with cruel satisfaction in her eyes, she had sneering glee on her face. The last sight he would ever see was the woman standing over him triumphantly, her red cloak billowing behind her, and bending her hooded head forward.

SEVEN

J enny was not sure that she wanted to go to the party. She thought maybe she wouldn't go. Then she thought maybe she would go. She didn't care either way. If she wanted to go, she would go. If she wanted to stay home, she would stay home. Whether she went to the party didn't matter.

Being sick in bed did not particularly inspire her to do anything. A blanket pulled up to her chin, her guitar in her lap, the strap pointlessly around her neck. She would not play the guitar or even touch it. Instead, she would sit there and stare at her poster of the Rolling Stones. Mick Jagger winked at her from within a cloud of smoke that seemed to rise from his mouth. A guitar leaned against his shoulder and a joint dangled between his lips. Keith Richards stood behind him, not looking as cool. Charlie Watts was drumming behind their heads and appeared to be the only one not high on something. The Rolling Stones were at their peak; soon, they would change irrevocably.

Not feeling like playing the guitar for a while, when she finally sat down to play the old instrument, her fingers were clumsy. She was used to this feeling. It was like being underwater, but what was different now was that her fingertips felt icy-cold. A regular feeling for her for longer than she could remember, but she also felt sadness now as well. The melancholy had dragged itself out of hiding at last, and it brought a lethargy with it. Her doctor had prescribed her new medication for ADHD, hoping it would lighten her mood a little. The pair had agreed on a mood stabilizer, and Jenny had been on it for two weeks now. She had not thought about getting the prescription until her father suggested it. Her father had said that she would benefit from a mood stabilizer and that she would need something to calm her down a little if she were going to focus on school. Two weeks ago, she had lost interest in everything; music, books, socializing. Now, she could feel herself becoming tired and withdrawn again. She kept hearing muffled sounds in her ears, like the noises of strangers talking behind thick doors or walls.

She had stopped taking her other medications because she didn't want to be reliant on them. She had quit taking Adderall and Vyvanse because they had made her feel horrible. They made her drowsy and uninterested in life. The side effects were too terrible for her to bear. Now she was off her medication and already she felt like a new person. Her energy was high, her head was clear, and she felt as if she could do anything.

She had been feeling better after her mother passed away last year, but now she was feeling worse. Her head hurt, and she had a headache that was coming and going, like a drill hammering into her brain, pressing against her skull, pushing outward, and then fading away again. She had been taking pain relievers to bring her headache down, but they weren't working anymore. A restful nap might help, but she didn't want to go to sleep right now. The bed was comfortable, but she didn't want to lie down. She would do her homework later; she didn't want to do schoolwork right now. The English textbook sat on the table and stared at her like an angry parent, who silently berated every move she made. She wanted English class to end so that she could get out; it might be better outside where nobody watched over her every move.

Looking at the poster of the Rolling Stones, she remembered when she had gone to see them when she was only five with her parents. The concert tickets were on her mind. She remembered the t-shirt that her father had bought her. She remembered her parents being excited, but she didn't remember them being excited about the concert.

Picking up her guitar, she strummed a chord. She played a few notes and then put the guitar down again with a disheartened sigh.

I should just go, she said to herself. Standing up, she went to the kitchen. She opened the fridge and leaned on the counter. Her father's beers were there. She grabbed one and twisted off the cap. She was not sure if this would work, but she figured that if she left it on the counter for a few minutes without drinking it, the carbonation would go back into the beer. Putting the top on the counter, she took a sip. The bubbly drink slid cold and wet into her mouth. She put down the beer, picked up another one, twisted off the cap, and plopped herself back down on her bed. This would not be as hard as she thought.

She grabbed her phone and texted Meg.

"Going to Dana's party, coming over?"

She waited for a response. She did not hear from Meg, so she put her phone down on the bed and looked at her guitar. Picking it up once again, she took a deep breath. Maybe if she played her guitar, she would feel inspired again.

The phone made its bleep-like sound, and she looked down.

"Might be late." Meg texted.

She texted back. "Ok."

"Dude Leon is going to be there... cute ASF!"

Looking at the message, she threw her phone down on the bed, not caring about Leon, and certainly not caring about him being "cute ASF." She wanted to play guitar and feel something, but she felt nothing.

She walked out of the room, down the hall, and into the living room. Her father was sitting on the couch. The television was on. He was watching a show about a barbeque competition.

"Hey," he said. "Are you going out?"

"I might go over to Dana's party," she replied.

"Ok," he said. "You should go. I'm just going to stay home."

Walking back to her room, hands clasped in front of her, she gave a quick nod and opened the door. She closed the door behind her and sat down in her comfortable computer chair. The music she listened to was blaring through the speakers, and she turned up the volume until it was as loud as it would go. She let the track pound through her body, shaking off the low mood that had followed her all day. As she did, her phone beeped, and a message appeared on the screen.

"Are you still going? I'm going to Dana's. Can we meet up?" Meg texted.

Jenny texted her back.

"I'm just staying home," Meg replied.

"Are you sure? I don't know if I want to go either."

"Can't go." She thumbed her cell phone and sent the message. The text was almost instantaneous. Her thumbs danced on the keypad as she typed.

"I'm almost here. Do you want to come?" Meg asked.

"If you promise not to talk to Leon, the lover boy all night," she replied.

"You break my heart, Jenny."

Shaking her head, the frown on her lips deepened. She strummed a chord, and a melodious sound filled the room. She added a melody on top of the chords, and then suddenly stopped playing. The notes faded into silence, leaving only the tinkle of the wind chimes hanging near the window. She set the guitar back down and picked up her phone.

"I can't believe you."

She thumbed the phone and read the response.

"I'm sorry!"

"Haha, I'm kidding. I am almost there. Meet you at the door."

Grabbing her keys, she ran out the door. She slammed it behind her and fumbled with the lock on the doorknob before she heard it click. Turning the ignition, she pulled out of the driveway and down the street. She drove as fast as she could down the roads, pressing down on the gas pedal and leaning into each curve in the road like a roller coaster. She went fifty miles per hour in a twenty-five-mile-per-hour zone. Turning right at the stop sign, she saw the house and pulled into the driveway.

She walked up the path that wound its way through the tall pines. The trees were covered in lush green leaves swaying in the wind. A stream bubbled to her right. The water gurgled and sloshed, and the stream bank was lined with soft, green moss and small white flowers. Smelling the scents of pine needles, roses, and wet bark, she swatted a mosquito away from her face. The ground quivered beneath her feet as she stepped over a tree root and onto a cedar porch larger and broader than any she had ever seen before.

She rang the doorbell, the laughter and music of the party flowing out onto the porch. A tall man with dark hair answered the door and welcomed her inside.

"Come on in," he said. The room was crowded with people, some standing, some talking in small groups. She could smell the alcohol in the air and pizza cooking in the kitchen.

"Jenny!" Dana called out.

"Dana!" she replied.

She was breathless. Her heart thudded in her chest. She ran into her friend's arms and was enveloped by the potent smell of flowers and her friend's soft hair. Dana's eyes were sparkling. Her blonde hair shone in the light. Her blue eyes were glittering with happiness. It was the welcoming arms of a good friend.

"Where's your coat?" she asked.

"I forgot it," she replied.

"You can wear mine," Dana said.

There were people everywhere, talking and laughing, smiling, and hugging one another.

Some moved in groups of two or three, holding hands or attached in a long chain of arms, like some sort of dance of affection and friendship. She saw a group of friends huddled around a bowl of punch, laughing together, and joking about someone named Phil who had spilled his drink the night before. She saw another group, separate from the first group, but laughing with just as much infectious joy. Despite resisting their laughter, she couldn't help but smile with them, smiling at Phil's misfortune and feeling joy for herself, as if she had been there with them and had spilled her own drink onto the floor.

"Hey, Jenny!" Charlotte called.

"Hey, Charlotte!"

"You want something to drink?"

She shook her head and Charlotte smiled and walked away. There were people everywhere drinking. Charlotte passed by her again and gave her a thumbs-up, causing Jenny to smile.

Some were standing in groups, talking to one another; others were dancing and swaying to the music, and some were making out on couches. The smell of fresh pot hung in the air and the sound of joints being sparked followed the smell into Jenny's nostrils. She could not stop herself from standing in the middle of the party and taking in the sight of the people. She did not want to go outside, and she did not want to go back home. She wanted to stay here.

She saw her friend coming back, and she smiled. Dana came up to her and put a wool coat around her shoulders. The coat came down to her knees. She could smell her friend's perfume on the coat. The smell of weed and the pine needles and the flowers and the perfume all mixed in with the sounds of the party. She breathed it all in deeply and sighed.

"We have to go find my date before he gets distracted."

"Have you seen Meg yet?"

"No, I haven't seen her. I'm going to try to find her."

"Ok..."

"Just go into the kitchen and go to the back, and you'll see Leon."

"What?"

"Leon, my date. He's in there talking to a couple of people. Just go up to him and start talking to him."

"He's your date?"

"He's so cute," Dana said.

"Ok," Jenny said.

Turning, she walked away from her friend and into the kitchen. She saw Charlotte in the kitchen and waved to her. Charlotte smiled at her and went back to the kitchen counter. Opening the icebox door, she took a can of beer out. She twisted the top open and took a long drink. After closing the door, she looked around the kitchen. There was a table with chips, salsa, and guacamole laid out. She grabbed a chip, dipped it in the guacamole, and brought it to her mouth. She chewed the chip and took another sip of beer. Looking around the kitchen, she saw a group of girls at the kitchen table sitting on tall bar stools holding tall glasses of red wine. They looked like they were in college.

She walked across the room to the table and sat down. Her butt sank into a soft leather seat, which groaned in protest as she settled into it. She felt the air conditioner waft cool air across her face and reached out to grab ice water from the table. Jenny's stomach grumbled as she drank, and as Leon walked in, she knew he would take care of that hunger for her. Her heart thumped with anticipation.

Leon walked over to where Jenny was sitting and kissed the girl next to her on the cheek. He turned to Jenny with a big smile on his face.

"Hey," he said, "I'm glad you made it."

Jenny blushed. She looked down at her hands and pushed her fingers together. She shook her head gently to tell Leon no, but she couldn't speak.

"How's it going?" Leon asked.

She didn't know what to say. Looking at him, she couldn't help but smile.

"It's going well," she said.

"Want a drink?" he asked.

"Sure," she replied.

Leon poured two glasses of red wine, then leaned against the counter and studied her carefully. He brought it to her and set it on the table before walking back to the counter. There were several small vases on the bar, each one holding a rose. He picked up a vase and pulled out a rose and brought it to her. She thanked him as he gave the flower to her, watching it lean to one side in his grasp, its stem flaring out like an erect penis. She blushed and looked down at it, inhaling its delicate fragrance. Her head spun as she took a sip of wine, her body relaxing as the wine warmed her insides. She swallowed the rest of it in one gulp, feeling more confident with each passing moment. She smiled at him, feeling both dominant and coy in his presence.

"What did Dana tell you?" he asked.

"That you were her date," Jenny replied.

Leon nodded.

"I asked her out," he said.

His straight, perfectly groomed hair brushed back from his face and well-kept sideburns. The hair looked so dark it was almost black, but it had blue and green highlights, like faded jeans. His eyes were light enough to be mistaken for blue, but with a spark of green hidden in their depths. He had a smooth face with a hint of shadows under his eyes. His skin was flecked with freckles across the bridge of his nose and under his eyes. Although he was young, his face carried the weight of the world's troubles. His chiseled smile was brilliant, like sunlight through tall trees. He looked like a man who had seen some things that no one should see.

She wished she could come up with something clever to say.

"That's awesome," she said.

Leon laughed, and she smiled.

"So, how long have you known Dana?" she asked.

"We went to high school together," he replied.

"Oh, wow. I didn't know that." She took a sip of wine. "I've lived here all my life."

"Where did you go to high school?" he asked.

"Here, at Pine Creek High," she replied.

"I didn't know that" he said as he shifted his feet.

"What?" she asked.

"That we went to the same high school."

"Oh..."

"How old are you?" Leon asked.

"I'm eighteen."

"I'm eighteen too."

"Oh, wow."

"Oh, wow?" Leon asked.

"I just mean that I would have remembered you," she replied.

Feeling her face grow hot, she looked away from him to avoid his gaze. She looked toward the pot smokers in the living room and saw them huddled around the coffee table with their pipes on the table. He laughed again and she smiled. Squeezing her shoulder, he went back to the counter to get another drink. She sat back in her chair and watched the party going on around her. People were playing games with dice and playing drinking games. One group was even playing Twister on the floor. An old goth song from the '80s was repeating "I'm dead... I'm dead"

Another group was making out. She looked at the young couple and imagined herself kissing a guy. Shaking her head, she sighed. She stood up and walked back to the counter. Taking another sip of her drink, she looked around the room. Two girls were sitting at a table with two guys. Seeing them putting their hands under the table and looking at the guys and whispering in one another's ears. She saw through their ruse and their little game. She finished her drink and put the glass down on the counter.

"I was wondering if you were going to finish that," Leon said.

She turned to look at him. She could see the vodka bottle he was holding in his hands.

"You want to go dance?" Leon asked.

"Ok," she smiled.

Putting his hand on her shoulder, he led her through the kitchen and into the middle of the living room. He placed his hands on her hips and leaned forward and pulled her toward him. She put her hands on his shoulders and looked into his eyes. They danced. They moved to the beat of the song and shimmied their hips. Jenny looked at the people in the room around them and watched them dance. She smiled and felt her phone buzz in her jeans. She ignored it.

It buzzed again. She reached down into her pants and pulled out her phone. She checked the message.

"Who's that?" he asked.

"It's my friend Meg," she said.

She looked at the message.

"Hey, I am at the door," Meg wrote.

"I need to go to the bathroom," Jenny spoke.

"Ok," Leon responded.

"I'll be right back."

She walked back to the kitchen and saw Charlotte sitting on a stool by the counter, talking to a couple of guys. Charlotte, who was wearing a short black dress, was laughing at something one guy said. Jenny walked toward the bathroom. She pushed open the door, which was wooden and carved. A chandelier cast a dim light over the space inside. The bathroom was bigger than a usual bedroom. It was marble-walled, and it even had a marble sink.

"I'm in the bathroom," she texted.

"Ok," Meg replied.

"I'm close," she texted back.

"Ok."

Looking at herself in the mirror, she patted her cheeks and turned her face to the side. She turned her face to the side and then up, stretching her cheeks. She pushed her lips out with her tongue and released a large exhale of air. Her face relaxed as she looked at herself in the mirror. Stretching out, she tilted her head from side to side, popping her jaw open and closed. Looking at herself in the mirror, she took a deep breath and relaxed. Her phone buzzed in her hand.

"I'm here."

"Ok."

Putting the phone in her back pocket, she took a deep breath. She heard the door of the bathroom open and looked over her shoulder to see Meg standing in the doorway with a bottle of wine in her hand.

"That took a minute," Meg said.

"I was admiring the room," she replied.

"Oh," Meg said.

They walked over to the table where the pot smokers were sitting. Jenny grabbed a chair and sat down opposite Meg without breaking her stride. She watched as a tall, bare-chested man entered the kitchen, and a smile curled across her face. He walked up to the counter and poured himself a drink. Meg pulled a joint from the ashtray and placed it between her lips. The long stem protruded from one side of her mouth. She pulled a lighter from her pocket, flicked it on, and held it to the tip of the joint.

"I've missed you," she said.

"I've missed you too," Meg replied.

Jenny put the joint to her lips and took a long pull. She pulled until it felt like her lungs would burst, then she held the smoke in her mouth and blew it from her nose. The smoke blew out and up in a ring that spread out, curling and dissipating. The smoke smelled of flowers and spices and happiness. Dust and smoke swirled in the air. She took a second deep breath and blew out more smoke, coughing from the feeling that her lungs were on fire, but laughing anyway.

"That was a good one," she said.

"Yeah, that was," Meg replied.

She looked at her friend and felt her heart swell up in her chest. She wanted to tell her friend all her feelings. Every single feeling in her chest and how she wished she could have been there to protect her from her father and her bullies and her fears. She wanted to tell her how she thought of only her when she was happy, how she was afraid for her when she was sad, and how she would give anything to make things right in her world. She pulled her phone out of her pocket and looked at her messages.

"I have to go outside," she said.

"Lame," Meg replied.

The night was cool, and the air was warm. The smells of home cooking and the sounds of families talking wafted through the open windows. Jenny could see the lights from the neighbors' houses beaming over the tops of the walls. She heard someone call her name. She turned around to see Charlotte. Charlotte waved to her from the other side of the fence.

Charlotte leaned closer to her and said, "Hey, listen."

Jenny was clearly enjoying herself. "What's up?" she asked.

"Well, since you're here and everything..." Charlotte started.

"Yeah?" Jenny asked.

"Well, I want to make sure that you are having a fun time and everything," Charlotte finished.

"Oh good," Jenny said.

"I'm having a really fun time."

"Well, I'm glad."

"I'm going to party the fuck out of this place," Jenny said, with enthusiasm in her voice.

"Oh good!"

"I really am."

Jenny laughed and threw her arms around Charlotte. She squeezed her friend and felt her heart swell in her chest. Her cheeks flushed, and she let out a long sigh. As she gripped Charlotte tightly, she suddenly released her, stepping back to look at Charlotte's face. She could see that Charlotte was crying. Her eyes were brimming, but no tears had spilled over yet. Jenny smiled at Charlotte, a genuine smile, one filled with warmth and love. She could feel the love swelling in her chest and spilling over into her hands that were resting on Charlotte's shoulders.

"What's wrong?" Jenny asked.

Charlotte didn't look up. "Nothing."

"You're crying," Jenny said.

"No, I'm not."

"Yes, you are."

"Nope. The fuck I am," Charlotte said softly, sniffling. The tears slid down her face, leaving snail trails of mascara. She was trembling.

"You're crying, and I want to know why," Jenny said.

Charlotte turned away from her. She looked at the crowd of people by the pool and felt her heart swell in her chest.

"I'm just really happy, I guess," she said.

Jenny looked at her friend and didn't know what to say.

They looked at each other and smiled. Charlotte wiped her eyes and turned her head away from her.

Jenny looked and saw her friends by the pool. They were laughing and talking. She saw the people in the kitchen. They were still talking and drinking. They were talking and laughing, and she realized that she wasn't missing anything but the people she loved.

"I'm going to change my hair," she said.

"What?" Charlotte asked.

She walked over to her friend and grabbed her by the shoulders. She looked into her eyes and smiled at her.

88

"I'm going to change my hair. I'm going to dye it blonde."
Charlotte leaned forward and hugged her.
"I'm so happy for you," she said.
Jenny hugged her friend back.
"I'm going to find a good job." Jenny continued.
"I know you will," Charlotte said.
"I'm going to move out of my house."
"I know you will."
Jenny let go of Charlotte and smiled at her. She was crying, and Jenny wiped her tears away.
"I'm going to be somebody."
"I know you will."
They looked at each other and smiled. Charlotte looked at her friend and wanted to tell her that the world was full of bad people and that you never really know who they were and that you must be careful and always look behind you. She wanted to tell her that people will hurt her, and people will use her, and people will betray her. That was what she wanted to tell her.
They stood in the backyard for a moment longer and looked at the people in the backyard.
"I'm going to be somebody," Jenny repeated.
"Of course, you will," Charlotte said.
"I'm a nice person."
"I know you are." Charlotte agreed.
"I'm not fucking around with people."
"I know that."
"I'm done with all of that," Jenny said, with a smile.
"Ok."

They looked at each other and smiled once more. Jenny walked through the kitchen and into the bathroom. She grabbed a towel from the towel rack and wiped the condensation from the mirror. Looking at her reflection, she brushed her hair with her fingers. Her hair fell around her shoulders. There was a towel and a glass. She looked at the mirror and the towel and she knew that nobody else was looking at her. Nobody was listening to her. She knew that nobody really cared about her. She knew she was all alone in the world.

She took a deep breath and dropped the towel onto the floor.

Walking out of the bathroom, she stepped over the towel, leaving it behind on the bathroom floor. She walked through the house, past her friends, as none of them looked up. She headed back to her car and drove home. Parking in her driveway, she made her way up to her room and fell asleep in minutes, dreaming of dancing with Leon.

EIGHT

T he call came in at nine while the sheriff was getting
ready for bed. The door to the bathroom was open
and he could hear the phone ring from where he sat on the
toilet. There was enough time for him to brush his teeth
and wipe his backside. Walking out into the bedroom, he
sat down on the edge of the bed and took off his shirt. He
picked up the phone and answered it.

It was Bob with county records.

"I have the address of someone who may have been a
witness to that murder," Bob said.

"Really? where?"

"408 Franklin Street, a single mother by the name of Barb
Nelson. She can meet you now."

"Thank you, Bob, I owe ya' one," he said.

"Anytime, bud," Bob replied.

"Leaving now."

He hung up the phone, put on a pair of pants, and got
into his car. He drove to the address Bob gave him. The

house was about an hour away from town. It was on a hill overlooking the creek. It was a pleasant building with a white picket fence around the yard and an extensive garden of flowers.

He pulled into the driveway and parked his car. He walked up to the house and knocked on the door.

He stood on the porch, surveying his surroundings. He heard dogs barking, the sound of children laughing, and a woman's voice. In the distance, a woman was trekking up the road towards him. She was wearing a flowing skirt that whipped around her legs as she walked. He took a deep breath in anticipation as she grew closer to him.

"Hello," she said.

"Hello," he replied.

"I'm sorry. I was in the woods with the children. "Kids, go inside and start getting ready for bed. I'll be right up."

"Ok Mom," a voice replied. He turned slightly and noticed two young children run into the house. He faced forwards again and saw that the woman was now standing in front of him.

"No worries," he said.

"You're here about the murder?" she asked.

"Well, sort of," he answered.

"Oh."

"You don't have to talk to me if you don't want to."

The woman stepped forward and held the door open. She led him into the house.

"I've been thinking about it," she said.

"Well, that's great."

She stepped a little closer to him. "I didn't want to until I was sure."

"Well, are you?" he asked.

"Yes," she whispered. She sounded nervous.

"You're sure?"

"Yes."

"Ok, well, I need to ask you a few questions. Can you go back in time and tell me what you saw?"

"I can try," she answered.

"Ok, good."

He followed the woman down the hall and into her kitchen. She motioned to a chair, and he sat down with a smile of gratitude. She sat across from him with an uncomfortable look on her face.

"I'm ready," she said.

"Ok, great" he said.

Opening his notebook, he looked up at her.

"Can you tell me what you saw?"

"I was driving down the road," she said.

"Which road?"

"The Ransom Road right behind Pencenpau Park."

"Ok," he said.

He wrote "Ransom Road" and "Pencenpau Park" in his notebook.

"I was driving down that road when I saw a girl," she explained.

"Ok."

"I pulled over to the side of the road and asked her if she was alright," she said.

"Who was the girl?"

"A young blond." She answered.

"Did she tell you her name?"

"No," she said. "She just said hello as she walked towards the park."

"Did she say anything else?"

"No," she said.

"What was she wearing?"

"A fancy high-end-looking dress and, I think, a long jacket."

"Anything else?"

"Yes, I remember feeling uncomfortable because I thought I saw a man waiting at the entrance and it was getting a bit dark."

He stared at the woman for a moment, watching the way her eyes lit up when she talked, the way her dark hair fell to the side. She looked like she was about to be sick.

"What did the man look like?" he asked. "Did you get a good look at him?"

"He was hard to see and dressed all in black," she replied. "He came through the trees and waited by the railing. I couldn't see him clearly."

"Ok," he said. "Tell me what happened next."

"I should have told you sooner," she remarked.

"I know, but it's ok."

"I just wanted to know for sure."

"What happened next?"

"The girl walked towards the park. When she got to the man, it looked like she told him something. He nodded, took something out of his pocket, and walked away."

"Did you see where he went?"

"No, as soon as I saw him, I drove away. It was getting dark, and my kids had to go to school the next day. So, I left."

"Ok," he muttered and looked down at his notes.

Looking back at the woman, he tried to think of the next question to ask her. He knew there were a few questions he should ask her. They were questions he had to ask. He reached into his pocket and pulled out a business card. He handed the card to the woman.

"Could you call me if you think of anything else, ok?" he said.

"Yes, I will."

"I really appreciate it," he said.

She nodded, and the sheriff stood up from the table.

"Thank you," he nodded.

He walked to the door and stepped out. His boots clumped on the wooden steps as he stepped up to his car. The heavy door creaked as he opened it and sat down inside, putting his flask between his legs and relaxing back into the seat. The smell of leather, sweat, and dirt wrapped around him like a memory, just like old times. Turning the engine on, he leaned back and sat there for a moment. There was a lot to think about. He put the car in drive and when he was out of eyeshot; he opened his flask and took a swig. The alcohol felt warm in his throat.

He drove home thinking about what the woman had said to him. He wasn't sure he believed her, but he wasn't entirely sure she was a liar either. He pulled into his driveway, parked, and sat in the driver's seat. After getting out of his car, he walked inside. Throwing his keys on the counter, he slumped down into his chair.

At the door, waiting for him, Leo wriggled and looked up at the sheriff. The sheriff crouched and rubbed his head.

"How was your day, buddy?"

Leo rolled over onto his back, and the sheriff rubbed his belly. He drank from the flask and closed his eyes. He finally climbed into bed and was asleep in a matter of minutes.

NINE

Waking up to the sound of his alarm clock, the sheriff opened his eyes to the sun gleaming brightly through the window. He stretched his arms out and pushed the button to turn off the alarm. The sun warmed his skin gently through the sheer curtain. He got up and went to the bathroom. His bare feet padded softly on the carpet while he pulled out his shaving kit, made a cup of coffee, and took it into the bathroom. He shaved and changed into his uniform. He took the coffee cup with him and placed it on the desk by his door. There were two images in his mind: one of a man drinking a cup of steaming coffee and shaving, and another of a man in uniform putting on a cap and adjusting it just so.

Grabbing his keys, he walked out the door. He locked the house and headed towards his cruiser. He opened the door and got in. Nothing happened when he turned the key. Pulling the key out of the ignition, he tried again. Nothing. The car wouldn't start despite his continued efforts. Getting out of the car, he popped open the hood. He was not a mechanic, but he felt like he could at least look at the engine. Peering under the hood, he felt something that was hot, but he couldn't see what it was. He grabbed his flashlight and looked inside the engine properly. He couldn't see much, but he could see that the radiator was in trouble. The water line was leaking. He had wondered when the car was going to break down and he was getting his answer now. He looked up and saw Leo standing by the car. The dog was looking at him, panting.

"Hey Leo," he said.

Leo walked towards him, sat down, and looked at him.

"What?" the sheriff asked.

Leo stood up, walked to the door, and looked out the window.

"I know you want to come with me, but you can't," he said.

Leo walked back towards him, looking at him.

"I am going to have to take a ride in my truck."

The sheriff put the flashlight down and took a drink from his coffee. The tailgate was open when he walked to the back of the car. He closed it grabbed his bag and his coffee and walked toward his truck. Leo was waiting by the driver's door.

"You can't come, buddy," he said. "When am I going to find time to take you out with all of this on my mind?"

The sheriff opened the driver's door of the truck and Leo jumped over to the passenger seat.

"Come on buddy, you need to go back into the house."

He ushered Leo inside. The old dog hobbled into the house and laid down on the floor. Heading back out, he locked the front door and strode to his truck. He threw his bag into the cab, hopped in, and started the engine.

The sheriff drove through the town and out the other side. He didn't know what to do with the car. He knew it shouldn't be parked on the street like that. The tow truck would have to come to pick it up. He pulled into the station and parked. After getting out of his truck, he unlocked the door of the station, and stepped inside.

He walked over to his desk carefully and sat down. Slipping his hat from his head, he placed it on his desk, then leaned back in his chair and stared at the ceiling. He took another drink from his cup and set it gently on his desk. The clock on the wall read 7:00 am. He was tired, but he knew he had many things to be doing. His desk was overflowing with papers and files that were piled high as mountains. His favorite heavy red pen lay on the desktop next to a stack of papers.

He picked up the pen and twirled it in his fingers and took a deep breath that he let out in a deep sigh. Shaking his mouse, he logged into his computer. As he waited for the screen to open, he scratched his head and looked at the clock. There wasn't much time to sort himself out and get ready for the day.

Sifting through his emails, he responded to a few of them. He opened his mailbox and looked at the paperwork that he had to sort through. A town hall meeting was going to be held this morning. He had asked the mayor to have a meeting with the homeowners to talk about the recent occurrences in the town. He leaned back in his chair and looked at the painting on the wall. It was a picture of his wife with her smiling face. She was beautiful and he would sometimes glimpse her face in the corner of his eye. She had enormous eyes, snow-white skin, and long, curly brunette hair. He looked at her long red dress and her lipstick-stained lips, which cracked into a smile. He wished she were here.

Sometimes he wished he could go back in time and do it all over again. He would stop the day when he and his wife walked down the aisle and kissed. Their eyes met, and they were in love. He often wished he could go back to that moment.

Taking a deep breath, he opened the first file. The pile of papers on his desk was taller than it had ever been. It was a daunting task ahead of him, but he had no choice. He had to get himself organized and get through this.

Going through page after page of the paper, he sorted, organized, and filed papers into their correct folders. He took a break, opened his window, and looked out at the town. Everything seemed so peaceful. It was a delightful sight to wake up to. He felt comfortable and at home in his town. He even felt at home in his own skin.

"I really could live here forever," he said to himself.

Looking at the clock, he took another sip of coffee. It was already past 9:00 am. He hadn't thought about breakfast at all.

TEN

The sheriff walked into the restaurant and looked at the menu. He wasn't particularly hungry, but he knew he had to eat, so he ordered the same thing he always ordered. A tuna sandwich with potato chips and a drink. The server smiled and told him she would be right back. She was young and pretty. He smiled, and she walked away.

Looking around the room, he saw a few familiar faces, but mostly strangers. He wondered what they were doing in a small town like his. He leaned back in his chair and crossed his legs, loosened his tie, and took a breath.

Rubbing his stomach, he looked at the road on the other side of the glass. The bakery truck was slowly making its way down the road. It was one of the few businesses that made its way up and down the streets.

He saw a beat-up old rusty van pull into a spot along the road and Rick Douglas get out and walk into the diner. Rick saw the sheriff and walked over to him.

"Rick," the sheriff said.

"Sheriff," Rick said, "what brings you out here?"

"I'm just out getting some breakfast," the sheriff answered.

"That's cool," Rick said. "I am here to meet my father; he should be pulling in now."

The sheriff looked up and saw the bakery truck pulling in behind the van.

"That's him," Rick said following the sheriff's gaze.

A large burly man with a bristly, salt-and-pepper mustache stepped out of the truck and stood there thinking. He looked around the parking lot and looked like he was trying to figure out where his son was.

"Over here, pops," Rick shouted, raising his hand in a half-wave.

The man looked up and approached his son and the sheriff.

"Sheriff," the man said.

"Hello Mr. Douglas," the sheriff said. "How have you been, sheriff?"

"Not bad," the sheriff said. "How about you?"

Rick's father walked up to his son and extended his hand to the sheriff. His hand was as big as a dinner plate and as rough as sandpaper.

"Not bad," he said. "You been keeping our town safe?"

"I am doing my very best," the sheriff said.

"Well, I guess that we'll leave you to it, sheriff. Gonna go get one of those famous giant pancakes they make!" Rick exclaimed in excitement.

The sheriff tipped his head. "Have a good day, guys."

"It's just Rick and thanks," he replied, tipping his head back.

Rick was a nice enough guy and he had never had a problem with him. He was the type that took care of his elderly parents. They were a little on the strange side, but overall, good people. It was something to admire in this world. The sheriff thought that people like that make the world go around and he figured these people must think the same way and keep their thoughts close to their hearts.

The server soon returned with his sandwich, interrupting his thoughts. She placed the basket on the table and walked away. He took a bite. The bread was soft and warm, the tuna inside was firm, and the chips had a nice thin layer of salt on them. The dill pickle was slightly sour, and it added some tang to the whole meal.

He took another bite of his sandwich and looked at the clock. It was almost 11:00 am. He knew he should get back to the station so he could get a few more things done and head to the town hall meeting.

Taking a sip from his water, he wiped his mouth with his napkin before putting it back down on his plate.

After finishing his food, he quickly paid the cashier, and walked out of the restaurant and into the street. He looked at the clock on the wall in the restaurant. It read 11:07 am. He was late for the town hall meeting. He hurried and got into his truck and turned on the radio. The song that was playing was one of his favorites. He took a deep breath and looked at the sky. The sun was bright, and the sky was clear. It was a perfect day.

Walking into the town hall, he looked at the clock on the wall. 11:20 am. There were already a few people sitting in the front rows of the room. They were catting quietly to one another. He could only imagine what they were talking about. He tried to step noiselessly so as not to disturb the rest of the people. He didn't want to be the center of attention. That wasn't really his thing, but he knew that people would want to hear about what was going on in their town.

Walking into the back of the room, he sat down in the last row near the door. Taking a deep breath, he glanced around the room. He saw the mayor sitting up front, who smiled and looked down at the podium.

He leaned back and stared at the ceiling. A few minutes passed before the door to the meeting room opened. More people were entering the room and taking their seats. The sheriff looked at the clock. It was 11:33 am.

The mayor stood up, stepped behind the podium, and started the meeting. He explained what was going on with the things that were happening in town. Shocked, the people wanted to know more. The talk went on and on and the sheriff got bored. He was impatient and wanted to get out of there because he never really liked meetings. He just wanted to get things done and be on his way.

Looking at his watch, the sheriff saw it was 11:53 am. He wasn't paying attention to the meeting anymore. There was a lot of yapping going on, which was irritating him. He finally decided that he had enough. Frustrated, he decided to just leave. He stood up and walked towards the door.

Unlocking it, he pulled it open and trudged outside. The sun was shining down on him, and it felt nice. He walked down the steps of the town hall and into the grass. It was wet, and the mud squelched beneath his feet. He continued walking down the street and stopped when he got to his truck.

As he approached the truck, sat down, and leaned back in his seat, he took a deep breath and watched the people go about their business. Closing his eyes for a moment, he relaxed. He felt so tired. His muscles were aching, and he wanted to take a nap.

Since he couldn't have a nap, he instead headed back to the station to get some things done before he went home. The truck roared to life and the enormous engine idled loudly and shook. The sheriff smiled; he loved the sound of his engine. He put it in gear and drove down the road.

He pulled up to the station and remained sat in his truck for a few moments. His shirt was drenched with sweat and his body was tired, but he needed to get a few things done. Opening his door, he stepped out and strolled inside. Madison greeted him.

"Hey sir, how did it go?" Madison asked. The sheriff stared at her and then looked around to see if anybody was listening.

Turning to face her, he leaned back in his chair and took a deep breath. Shifting his weight, he said. "It was just some stupid talk, like usual. I don't understand why people must carry on like that. The mayor sure likes to listen to himself fucking blab."

She sighed in response. "You're right. I hate politics."

Madison took a deep breath and pulled out the files that were given to her earlier. She handed them to the sheriff and then stepped back.

"What is this?" the sheriff asked.

"That's the list of everyone that's been coming in and out of town. We should find out what they're doing here and who they are," she said.

Nodding, the sheriff said, "Thank you. Give me a minute."

Madison left the room and headed back to her desk to answer some calls.

The sheriff looked over the papers that Madison had given him, reading them repeatedly. He wrote some notes on a piece of paper and then threw them in his drawer. Sitting back in his chair, he closed his eyes. He was so exhausted, and he just wanted to sleep.

The sheriff woke up to the sound of Madison's voice. He didn't know how much time had passed, but it felt like he had been sleeping for hours. Pinching his arm, he realized he wasn't still asleep, and it was really happening. Madison was shaking him.

"Sheriff!" she yelled, "Get up!"

Rubbing his eyes, he asked, "What do you want?"

"There's another body," she said. "We need to go now!"

The sheriff looked up from his desk aghast. "Another one? Dammit to hell!"

"They found it just outside the mill, in the woods." She spoke.

"When was the body found?" the sheriff asked.

"About thirty minutes ago," she clarified.

The sheriff stood up and walked towards the door. Madison opened it for him, and the pair marched outside. The sheriff got into his truck and put it into gear. The engine roared as he turned on the radio. Some old classic rock music was playing, and the sheriff groaned. He hated this music, but it was Madison's favorite.

He drove to the mill and found a few other county police cars and an ambulance parked near the entrance. He stepped out of his truck and walked into the mill.

The room was dark, and it smelled like mold. He walked into the back and found the few county police officers that had been called there. Madison walked up to them and handed the sheriff a pair of rubber gloves. He took them from her and walked into the room with the other officers.

The body was lying next to a pile of wood. Someone had ripped his stomach open, from his sternum to the bottom of his ribs. An arm hung limp, touching the ground.

There were parts of the body that looked like an animal had eaten it; the rib cage, bones, and tendons showing through ripped-open flesh. The sheriff winced as he circled it with intrigue.

Madison followed him and stood next to the coroner. The two of them observe the body.

The coroner pulled out a camera and snapped a few pictures of the body.

"Hey Walker," the sheriff said.

The coroner turned around, looked at the sheriff, and nodded.

"Same guy?" the sheriff asked.

"Not sure but looks it. We'll have to do an autopsy, and then I'll know for sure."

"Who found the body?"

"A little girl found him. She said that she had been following something in the woods and it led her here."

"Where is she now?" the sheriff asked.

"She went home with her mother. I told her father to come down here and talk to us."

"How long do you think it will take?"

"A few hours at the most."

The sheriff nodded. He and Madison walked out of the mill. As they walked up the sunny dirt path, Madison put on her sunglasses.

"Same thing, no organs and cut open?" she asked.

"Looks like we have ourselves a real psycho here," she said, squinting up at the sun.

"Well, I'm going to go talk to this girl's father," said the sheriff. He pinched the bridge of his nose and shut his eyes, the headache from last night still reverberating through his skull. He just wanted a drink.

"I'll be at the station going over the files we got from the mill," Madison decided. The sheriff nodded, then walked over to his truck and got in. He took the key out of the ignition, placed it in his pocket, and then opened the door.

He stepped out, walked around the back of his truck, and took out a cigarette. Lighting it, he leaned back against the truck and adjusted his hat. He inhaled the smoke and let it flow out of his mouth and nostrils. His eyes were squinting from the smoke, but he did not care.

The girl's father was standing by the county police, talking. He dropped his smoke onto the ground and crushed it under his boot heel, then headed over.

He extended his hand to the father to shake it, but the man just looked at it.

"I'm the sheriff. Can I ask you a few questions?" he asked.

"Yeah," the man replied.

"What's your name?" the sheriff asked.

"Edmond Daniels."

"What did your daughter see?" the sheriff asked.

"Emily said she saw something in the woods, something strange. She said it was tall and dark, and that she didn't know what it was. I guess it came from behind her and she turned around. She said it looked like a man, but it wasn't human. It had a strange face, with red eyes and..." Edmond stopped.

"What?" the sheriff asked.

"Nothing... I just want to find this thing and kill it," Edmond said.

"Your daughter was in the woods?"

"I told her not to go in there! I told her. We live right behind the mill, and she is always so damn curious."

"I understand." the sheriff said.

"I don't want her to see... whatever it is again," said Edmond.

"We'll keep her away from the crime scene. She won't be able to see anything," he spoke.

"Come with me. I'll take you to her."

They walked up to Edmond's small white house. Then, the sheriff went inside and sat down on the couch. Edmond was just shrugging off his coat, but he looked up with a somber expression, a mixture of grief, fear, and anger. There was a photo album and a small bowl that had some keys in it on the coffee table. The sheriff picked up the bowl and looked at the keys in the bowl. The jingling sound of the keys filled the room.Edmond's wife was in the kitchen sobbing, and the sheriff could hear her muffled whimpers. He looked at the photos. The pictures were of the factory, the small houses and stores, and the forest.

The sheriff looked up at Edmond. "Nice place. I see you guys live near the woods."

"Yeah, it's our backyard."

The sheriff looked back at the photo album. There were pictures of Edmond working at the mill. The sheriff could tell Edmond was smiling in the pictures. It brought a sort of sorrow to the sheriff. He couldn't help but think about what happened at the mill.

"This is terrible," the sheriff said.

Edmond looked nervous. "Our neighborhood is changing."

The sheriff looked at the pictures again. There was one that showed Edmond, his wife, and Emily, who was about seven or eight. The sheriff could see that Emily was his daughter. She had grown up. In the photo, she was all smiles, with her teeth shining through, but her eyes looked sad. There were more photos of the family, at some sort of party or ceremony, but no one was smiling.

The sheriff looked back up at Edmond, who was standing by the door, shuffling his feet back and forth.

A little girl, little more than eight, came into the living room with her sobbing mother. Her eyes were wide and streaked with tears. Her pink bow was a little crooked. A strand of her dark hair had fallen in front of her face, and she pushed it out of the way with her tiny hand.

The sheriff stood up and approached her. She was shaking.

"Emily?"

"Yeah... that's me," she said in a quiet voice.

"My name is Sheriff Cross; I understand you were the one who found the body?"

"I didn't mean to!" she said in a loud whisper.

"It's alright, there is nothing to worry about."

Emily wiped away the last of her tears and bit her lip.

"Can you tell me what happened?" the sheriff asked.

"I was playing in the woods, and I heard something. I thought it was a bear or a bunny or something, but it wasn't. It was this person. He came out of nowhere. I think it was a monster. It was so tall, bigger than dad. It had these strange eyes. I don't know, they were red and stuff.... in funny-looking clothes..."

Emily stopped. She put her hands over her mouth and started sobbing again. Her mother held her, trying to comfort her.

"What kind of clothes Emily? What color?" he asked.

"It was all black. It looked like a cape or something."

"Did you see any of his face?"

"Just his eyes and..."

Emily cried again; her mother sobbed along with her.

"What?" the sheriff pressed gently.

"Its hands..." she whispered.

"What about them?"

"Well, they were kind of like a skeleton. It had long fingers, like in the movie."

"What movie?" he asked.

"One of my friends showed me one movie that has a monster in it."

"Oh, ok, there is no such thing as monsters honey," he told her.

Emily began to cry again.

"I know, but I saw it. I'm not lying," she said between sobs.

"I know, sweetie. It's ok."

"Can you tell me what happened when you saw the dead man?"

Emily's eyes shifted, looking at her mother. She was clutching her shirt and clinging to it.

"I was scared and ran to the mill where daddy says not to go but I sometimes do anyway. I thought it was someone sleeping."

"And you knew that?" he asked.

"Yeah, I could see it. His eyes were open, that made me even more scared, so I ran home as fast as I could."

"Thank you for talking to me, Emily."

He stood up and shook her father's hand. "Thank you for your time."

"We'll be here if you need us."

The sheriff walked out of the living room, through the front door, and closed it softly. He walked back to the mill, his hands deep in his pockets, his head down.

When he got back to the crime scene, the body was still there, covered by a sheet. He didn't want to look at it. With a sigh of contempt, the sheriff knelt. He grabbed the sheet and moved it, revealing the dead man. The sheriff had known the man. He was an older resident of the town who had been living alone since he lost his wife to cancer a few years ago. He had been talking about going to Florida, but he didn't have enough money. For as long as anyone could remember, he was around Pine Creek. He had been homeless for years now. Pine Creek had its small share of homeless people. More so since the coal mines had closed. The company had dug out every mountain as fast as they could and there was nothing left. They got shut down for good after a bad rockslide killed ten men. The accident still haunted the town.

And now, there just was not enough work for everyone.

The sheriff stood up and grabbed his radio.

"Dispatch, this is Sheriff Cross. I have ID'd the body, it's Lemont Bradley. Get a team out here and a medical examiner. He has been dead for a while, at least a couple of hours."

"Roger that, Sheriff."

The face was completely mangled as if a wild animal had chewed on it. He looked closer at the man's face.

"What the hell?"

He took a few steps back and stared at the body, eyes widened. He was missing part of his nose, his left ear, and both eyes. The sheriff could see that his teeth were missing, too.

"What is this?" he hissed.

The sheriff knelt back down and got up close. He could smell the decay. It was as if the man had been dead for weeks. The sheriff could see dried blood. He moved the sheet up more. The man was missing the inside of his mouth. The sheriff was disgusted. He stood up, but next to the body was a small pile of teeth.

He picked them up in a small plastic bag. He took one more step back and looked around him at the forest.

He knew he had to meet with the coroner later about this, but that he also had to call the FBI. He took his phone out and dialed.

"Hello."

"Hi, this is Sheriff Cross. I need to speak to an agent."

"Hold on one moment." a voice said.

The sheriff could hear many voices in the background.

"Agent Hasler speaking, what can I do for you, Sheriff?"

"I need an agent in Pine Creek, the mill."

"What is it?"

"There's another dead body."

"What do you mean?"

"It looks like the man was ripped apart. Half-eaten by animals after lying here for hours. Probably a coyote."

"Ok, give me the address."

"I'm at the mill, in Pine Creek."

"Ok, I'll be there."

"Wait, there's one more thing."

"What?"

"It could be nothing."

"Ok."

"The man, who I think is homeless, is missing his teeth on all his organs are missing... completely gutted."

"Ok."

"And his eyes and his nose. There is also a small pile of teeth next to him."

"Your point?"

"I don't know, just something is really weird here. Could use your help."

"Alright, I'll be there in the next hour."

"Great."

The sheriff hung up the phone and walked back to his truck. He had to tell the coroner and get back to the station. He opened the door and sat down. His eyes were narrowed, and his brows were furrowed. He started the truck and drove back to the station, thinking only about the teeth, the ripped apart face, and the missing organs.

The town of Pine Creek was a quiet town. It had a population of three thousand; he knew almost every one of them. The sheriff reached the police station. It was empty. There was a single lamp on the desk, a large one that sat in the middle of the room. Covering the walls were pictures from the town, from the opening of the mill to the mining accident. He stood in the middle of the room for a moment. It was quiet. The only sound was the ticking of an old clock. Everything felt too quiet for him. An ominous feeling grew in his stomach. He'd never felt it before, but he knew it wasn't good. He shook his head and made his way to the door behind the desk.

He walked into the hallway and opened the door to his office. On the left was a large window. It looked out to the county and Pine Creek. Sitting down at his desk, he turned on the computer. He started typing a report and sent it to his email. He did not know if the FBI would even come, but he figured he would at least try. After he emailed, he sat back in his chair and stared at the ceiling.

He felt like he was forgetting something, but he could not for the life of him remember what it was. As he was about to get up and get a coffee from the break room, they turned the tv in the corner on.

The local news came on and, a blonde woman started talking, "Today, in Pine Creek, a fifty-three-year-old man was found dead at the mill. They have identified him as Lemont Bradley, a homeless man who has been in Pine Creek for over twenty years. According to the sheriff, the cause of death is unknown, and the FBI and the coroner are currently on the scene. The sheriff said that he saw the body and there were unusual circumstances surrounding the death. We have a reporter on the scene. Jordan?"

The sheriff stared at the tv as a young man stepped in front of the camera, a serious expression on his face, "Yeah, Jennifer. It is an unusual death for sure, described as gruesome by the sheriff. The body is in the middle of the clearing, behind the mill. I can see the body has been covered with a sheet, but there is clearly an outline of the victim underneath. The police are refusing to comment on the death. We can see that they also cordoned the mill off. The sheriff told us that the FBI and the coroner were on the scene but gave no further details. We will keep you updated. Back to you, Jennifer."

The sheriff glanced at the tv again. The young man was gone, and the pretty blonde woman was back.

"Thanks, Jordan. We will keep you updated on this story here at Channel 33 of Pine Creek!"

The sheriff sat back in his chair, head lolling, eyes closed. His brow was lined and furrowed, but his breathing was steady. His mind raced.

"Fuck me," he muttered to himself.

ELEVEN

At school, Jenny wore her favorite pants, a pair of red jeans. They were a little tight and the color was a little bold for school, but it was Monday, so she felt like looking a little different today. She did her hair up with a fancy hairband, one that she had not worn in a while. It had been in the back of her locker, forgotten. The elastic was just stretching out, but it would hold. She liked the way it felt, like something old and forgotten that you find and suddenly is brand new again. She had also found an off-brand perfume in the back of one of her drawers, a gift from her grandmother during the summer. Whether the smell was nice, she just enjoyed thinking about her grandmother when she wore it. It made her feel safe and warm. She didn't have time to think about these things very often.

She'd also received an invitation to the formal from Leon after the party, which was so unexpected. They didn't know each other well at all, but still, it had somehow happened. She was giddy for a change. She also could not get Leon out of her mind. She knew she should not think about him too much. He'd asked Dana out too, so she wasn't sure if he liked her or the idea of having two girls at once.

That is all he saw her as, but she knew there was more to herself, and even if there wasn't, this was only high school. What mattered was graduating, getting into college, and having new experiences, and meeting new people. Still, she could not help but care about what he thought about her. It mattered to her what he thought of her. It mattered why she hadn't gotten around to calling him back yet or saying yes, for that matter. She hoped he would ask her to the dance again. It wasn't even a date, technically, just two friends going as friends. It would be nice because maybe then they could go somewhere after and do something together, something that wasn't planned, but just random acts of impulsive teenage happiness.

Jenny checked her phone before she left for school. Leon had sent her a text.

"Hey, sorry I missed you. I'm at the store buying some stuff for the homecoming dance. You should come over to my house after school and we can do something. I'll be waiting!"

She had not replied yet because she did not know what to say to him. She did not want to sound too eager, too excited, too interested, too uninterested, too nervous, or too ready to hang out.

She really wanted to go, but she could not think of a good excuse. She did not want to just get out of school and go to his house, but she also wanted to be with him, to explore the idea of being friends with him.

As Jenny left last period class, she noticed Dana and Lee having a conversation by the lockers.

Lee was a new kid at the school, which caused a lot of gossip among the students. Most of them thought he was a weirdo, and they didn't want to talk to him. He wore strange clothing, had weird hair, and he never seemed to be in any of his classes. It seemed he was always in the library, the cafeteria, or the bathroom, but never outside with other students. He was tall and skinny but had a weird bald spot on his head. He always carried a pen and a notepad with him in his back pocket, which he was always doodling in and making images of people and faces. Sometimes he would even write short stories and leave them on his desk.

He was friends with Dana. They did the same type of things, were in all the same classes together, and everyone said he had been her boyfriend. They had no evidence of that. Despite that, the gossip was spreading like a disease throughout the school. Jenny thought Lee was okay; she had talked to him a little in the cafeteria, but he was silent, and he didn't make eye contact. She felt sorry for him because she had seen no one gets bullied as much as he did.

She went to her locker and turned the lock. She took her bag and coat out of it, then grabbed her cell phone and looked at Lee and Dana. Then she turned around and took a picture of them. She smiled as she took it, not knowing why, but she did.

The picture was blurry when she looked at it. She was not sure why she took it; she just did and now she had a picture of Dana and Lee. The two of them looked close. Jenny smiled to herself and thought, maybe they are dating.

Then her phone light blinked. There was another text from Leon.

"What's up?" he said.

"Nothing."

"What's the matter?"

"Nothing."

"Come over to my house after school."

"Can't, sorry." she messaged back.

"What?"

"I can't."

"Why not?"

"I have responsibilities here."

"What responsibilities?"

"I have to babysit my little brother."

"Oh. Ok."

"What do you want me to do? My mom said I could go out with my friends tonight and she will watch him, but I have to babysit him first."

"I have homework to do."

"Sure. No Prob."

Jenny put her phone in her pocket. Her phone felt heavy and hot in her pocket. She did not know why she did not just go over to his house. It was crazy what she was doing. She wanted to go to his house so badly, wanted to see him, wanted to spend time with him, but she did not want the rumors.

She was now standing directly in front of Dana and Lee. Dana was looking at her intently like she was saying something to her. Jenny was going to ask her what she was doing, but she did not want to get involved. She wanted to get out of this whole Dana and Lee thing.

She walked away to the locker room and got changed. She put on her long, black coat and left school, and walked to her car. It was cold outside, and she was happy about it. She was glad that she was wearing her pants and a shirt. Some of the other girls from school were wearing summer clothes, and it was chilly today.

The sun shone through the clouds, and she could feel it. It felt like it was about to shine fully, but it never did. The tease was always there. It would shine for a few seconds, but then it would turn back into a hazy, gray sky covering the world in shadow. And that's the way it was with Jenny. Was just a tease. She could feel it, but she would never do it. She was always going to do something when the time was right, but she never did.

She got in the car and sat there. She put her key in the ignition and turned it. The radio was on. She listened to the DJ talk.

"Sunny Pine Creek! It is 4:00 pm here, and the sun is shining, it is a bit chilly, but a good day for a swim! There is always something to do in Pine Creek!"

She turned off the radio and pulled out of the driveway. Her little brother was at home, waiting for her so that he could eat dinner. Her mother was at work. She drove through the streets of the town and up the hill to the top of the mountain and then down to Leon's street.

Parking her car in his driveway, she turned off the ignition, turned it back on, and then turned it off again. With a sight, she put the keys in her pocket.

She got out of the car, walked to the door, and rang the doorbell. No one answered. She waited for about thirty seconds, no answer. She was not sure why she even came here. She felt bad because she had to tell her little brother a lie and that she was staying late at school. She rang the doorbell again.

She could hear the wind blowing through the curtains and the trees and the tall grass. There was a squirrel in the backyard, running up a tree. A sound of the doorknob being clicked and then turned. The door opened.

Leon was at the door. He smiled, and he had a bit of rosy blush on his cheeks. He had jeans on, a white t-shirt, his hair was a little messed up, and he had a wolf's tooth necklace around his neck.

"Hey." He spoke.

"Hi."

"Come in."

The house was filled with paintings of beautiful women, flowers, and mythological creatures. A lot of them were the style of the Renaissance period, with curly hair and curvy bodies, hats with veils; others in abstract styles that seemed to move before her eyes. From the kitchen, she could see his dining room table and a long chandelier hanging from the ceiling. It cast its light all over the room. She could tell there was no one home because the house was so quiet. The smell of freshly baked cookies, sunflowers, and other strange flowers she had never smelled before was filling the air.

Leon was looking at her, smiling. He was doing it so widely; she thought his face was going to get stuck that way. Feeling awkward, she ran a hand through her hair, looked at the floor, and then looked up at the ceiling. Then she looked back at him, and he was still there. His gaze was still fixed on her, and he was still smiling brightly.

She walked through the living room. She passed a black piano and a white couch. The wood floor in the hallway made the click-clack of her heels echo throughout the house. She could smell the flowers and the paint and the pencils and the book paper. This had to be one of the largest homes in Pine Creek.

Leon walked behind her, his shoes also tapping loudly against the wooden floor. He was warm, solid, and real. She could feel him walk behind her. The sound built up inside her head until she had to turn around.

She put her coat on the floor, her bag on the table, and she sat on the couch. The cats jumped over her legs, and she held out her hand. The cats started rubbing against her hand and her arms, their eyes half-lidded in pleasure.

"So, how was school?"

Jenny thought about it for a second.

"It was nice. Hey, this is one fancy house you have here," she observed. It was nice. She had spent her whole life in a trailer, and this place was huge. The walls were stone bricks, polished to a silvery sheen, and the room was cozy and well-lit. Elaborate tapestries interwoven with ancient symbols lined the walls. The furniture was built of thick wood with interlocking geometric patterns that spiraled to the floor.

The colors all blended but were still beautiful.

Leon smiled.

"Yeah, I guess so."

He offered her some cookies he'd been making. Jenny took one and bit into it. It had a crispy outside, and a soft inside and was so delicious, that she ate five in a row. She ate one, then another, and then two more, until the only one left was the biggest one. She was still hungry, so she ate that one, too.

Leon laughed at her.

"You're a real cookie monster, aren't you?" He chuckled.

Jenny laughed and smiled because she could not believe how nice he was being. She thought he was going to be a jerk. She was still nervous, but she was trying to hide it.

"Who do you live with?" she asked.

"My folks, but they aren't here much, so I pretty much live by myself. I like it that way."

"Really?" Jenny asked.

Leon went to the kitchen, got her a glass of water, and brought it back to her. He handed it to her, and she took long sips. She could feel the coolness of the water cascading down her throat, the beads of water forming on her lips.

She coughed a little, and she laughed.

"Thanks," she said.

"Welcome, hope you live after that cough!" Leon said, laughing with her.

"Ha. Do you always bake cookies?"

"Only when I have a guest over," he admitted.

Jenny laughed again.

"I'm so sorry. I hope I'm not keeping you from something."

"No, no, you're fine," he said.

Taking her water back from him, she took another drink. Her eyes scanned his furniture, his paintings, his cats, and his huge silverware collection. She felt like a little girl in a dollhouse.

She got up and walked towards the painting of the blonde woman with the big breasts, big butt, and the big blonde curls.

She looked at it for a second, then at him.

"Is that a Vermeer?" she asked.

Leon coughed.

"Wow, you know a lot about art," he said.

Jenny looked at the painting again, then at the other paintings in the house. She thought about how she had never seen this many paintings in her life, or anything so fancy or beautiful. She thought about how she wished she could live in a place like this.

"So, are you an artist?" she asked.

"Yeah, I guess so," he said.

She looked at the painting again. The blonde woman in the painting was wearing a dress that was strapped around her back and her neck, and it had a very loose top. She was wearing a hat that looked like a flower. She had a fan in her hand, and she was standing in the middle of a garden.

Jenny looked at Leon.

"Really?"

"Yeah. Art's just something I like to do," he said.

She was making him nervous.

"What do your parents do?" she asked.

"They're doctors."

She sat down next to him on the couch.

"I really love this painting. It's so pretty. You can tell that she's happy. You can tell she's free by her expression. I love how the light's coming from the windows too. I love it."

"You know," he said, "that's my favorite painting, too."

She laughed.

"That's so funny. I love all these paintings, man. This one's got so many colors and I love the way the cats are looking at me. I love the way it's painted. The way everything looks is real to me. It's beautiful."

Leon laughed. "Thanks," he said.

Jenny's heart was racing. She wanted to kiss him and wanted to be with him.

She looked at him. He smiled at her. She smiled back.

She looked into his green eyes, so dark, and felt his warmth through his t-shirt. She felt his love through his eyes, and she felt his spirit through his chest.

She leaned towards him; her eyes closed. She could feel his hot breath and his stiff lips. Her hands found their way to the soft bed of his hair, and she pulled him closer. She took in the earthy scent of him and could feel his tongue gently pressing against her mouth. He had a hand on her back, strong and protective and full of love. She wanted to be so close to him that there was no space between where he ended, and she began.

They took each other's clothes off without taking their mouths off each other. They made love, sucking, biting, and licking. Slick with sweat and sex, they slid against each other's bodies. They held each other tight, arms around waists, necks, and shoulders, skin to skin, heart to their chest.

Afterward, she lay next to him. She did not want to leave him, but she had to go. She wanted to hold him forever, but she knew her brother was waiting for her.

"I have to go," she said.

"I know," he said.

"I have to go home but I want to be here."

"You should."

"Please, can I stay?"

"Well, I don't mean here, here. But of course, you can stay here. I mean, with me," he said.

Jenny laughed. She could feel her heart beating and she could feel him holding her close. She could feel him, his love, his arms wrapped around her.

"Of course," she said.

"I'm going to hold you like this forever." He kissed her. "Forever."

She got up and dressed. She picked up her purse and started back to the front door.

She turned around and looked at him.

"Thank you," she said.

"No, thank you," he said.

He walked her to the door, and she opened it.

"I really like you," she said sweetly, her cheeks covered in a faint blush.

Leon smiled.

"I really like you, too," he responded, his lips curling up in a smile.

"I'm going to see you again, right?" she asked.

"Yes, baby, I'm never going to let you go."

And with that, she walked out the door, and he closed it behind her. She looked around and sighed, glancing over the busy street. She knew there would be more people with open arms if she wanted them, but she was content with where she was, and who she was with. As she drove out of the subdivision, she saw the sunset and heard the radio station's pop music. The song was catchy and fun, and she sang along with it. She remembered happy times in her life when the lyrics reminded her of who she was. The sun set slowly over the town, a warm blanket of orange, red, yellow, and brown. The clouds were wispy and faint around the edges. She felt as if she was dancing in the sky as she took it all in.

TWELVE

The day had been hell, and Madison was exhausted. Another body found meant for sure there was a serial killer. The sheriff had called in the FBI for help, but the FBI was no help. They were sending in some profiler, but Madison knew what it was going to be. It was going to be another one of those cases where the FBI would show up a few days too late and then tell them what they already knew. She did not want to deal with it.

The whole town was buzzing with news and gossip. The town never usually had anything interesting happen. It was a one-traffic light railroad town that was far enough away from whatever city was close by that it didn't matter what happened there. Out here, the only people who mattered were the government officials, who knew better than to cause the residents any agitation. The government officials were always polite, and the residents of the town were always polite back to them.

130

Whatever happened inside this bubble stayed inside it, right? Still, everyone in town knew there was more beyond their borders. They knew about all the traffic jams in the cities and about all the people who traveled from city to city, state to state in search of work or a better life or just something different from what they had known before.

People from out-of-town told stories about places where cars got sent into space and they invented things every day, and everyone else thought about what it would be like to live in those places. But no one tried going there anymore because they, too, had turned into the same type of place as where they used to be. The only thing that was different now would be how expensive everything was. Now they would have a longer commute, higher rent, and everything else in their lives would be harder because they would not speak the language, know how things were supposed to work, or have anyone to help them along. Their children would not do as well in school, because they would imagine themselves in some other place instead of paying attention to the place they were currently in, and their grades would slip. They wouldn't get into college, and then they wouldn't get a good job. All their effort would have been for nothing because all they'd known was here, and there would be nowhere else for them to go.

All of this meant that the FBI's Behavioral Analysis Unit would take over the investigation. The press had been all over the Sheriff's office.

They interviewed Madison and asked her questions about the scene. Her questions were about the other bodies. They asked her questions about the clothes the victims had been wearing and about the items that were missing. They asked her questions about the killer, even questions about her life.

This was a small town filled with good, hardworking people. A killer scared them. The killer might be one of them. And as the townsfolk walked down the streets and crossed the roads, their minds turned to the killer, like a wind that howls throughout the night. Their thoughts turned in circles and zig-zagged like lightning, and the people were not sure who to trust or what to do next. It was a fear that drifted from person to person, and it sat inside each of their homes like a dark spirit. It was visceral and thick, like warm syrup oozing from a bottle. If you tried, you could touch it, feel it, taste, and smell it. And it stunk.

Madison turned on the shower and waited for it to warm up. She took off her clothes and wrapped a towel around herself. She had to get out of the house. Her boyfriend had already left for work. She'd not wanted to get out of bed. Even though they were such different people, she still loved him. Her phone buzzed, but she ignored it. A moment later, it buzzed again.

It was the sheriff. This was a call she'd hoped to avoid.

"Hello, Sheriff," she spoke into the phone.

"Hey, I just wanted to let you know that the FBI profiler is here. I'm going to show him the crime scene and then I'm going to introduce him to you and the rest of the team."

"Is this the same profiler that everyone's been talking about on the news?"

"Yes, I'm afraid so," he answered.

"Great. I just want to go on record as saying I don't want any fucking feds in on our case. The assholes from the city look down on us, sir."

"I know, Madison. I know."

"You want to tell me what the profiler's name is?"

"It's Liam Porter. He's a good man. I've worked with him before. He's lived nearby in Hawthorn for years. He knows our town. He knows the people. He's not full of himself. Just come in with an open mind, ok?"

Sighing, she said. "Fine, whatever."

"I'll see you soon."

Madison hung up. She didn't want to see the FBI. She didn't want to deal with them.

She was ready to step into the shower when her phone rang again, she looked to see the sheriff's contact pop up once more.

"Yeah, Sheriff?"

"He's here. He is standing in my office waiting for you."

"Great. Tell him I'll be there in a minute."

"OK, I will let you go."

"Alright, see you soon."

Madison hung up the phone. This did not sound promising. The sheriff was never in a rush.

The sheriff had been called to the scene, and he was directing traffic. He waved everyone down to his side of the street, directing them toward the curb with a huge, black-gloved hand. A few minutes later, Madison pulled up to the scene. She hopped out of her car and turned to lock it. The scorching sun beat down on her neck, making her ponytail damp with sweat. She crossed the street and approached the sheriff, careful to step around a police car that had pulled up right in front of her new Audi. It was a black sedan with tinted windows and shiny rims. Right now, it was surrounded by several police officers. She recognized the kid about to be escorted home by his mother. The boy's face was dotted with freckles and his cheeks were flushed red from the sun. He looked ashamed as he walked past her and got into the backseat of his mom's car.

The FBI profiler stood in front of the mill. He stood a safe way off the road across dirt and grass. The immense building loomed dark and foreboding. He looked to be at least six feet tall, with broad shoulders, dark hair, and dark eyes. His hair was messy, and he had a scruffy face. He wore a long-sleeved plaid shirt, jeans, and cowboy boots. He didn't look like the feds she had seen on TV and in the movies, nor any she had met before.

Madison walked up to him across the dirt and grass.

"I'm Deputy Madison Colby," she greeted, extending her hand.

"I'm Liam Porter. It's nice to meet you."

He had a charming smile, and his eyes were warm. He seemed nice.

He had a slight southern accent, which was unusual for this part of the country. His handshake was firm and confident. He was wearing a large black coat with a black scarf around his neck. She looked at him and he smiled.

"If you'll follow me, I'll show you around," she said.

"That would be great, thank you."

Madison walked him around the scene of the crime. She told him what they had found and what they had ruled out. She told him about the victims and the missing items.

"What do you think it means?" Porter asked.

"It means there's a serial killer." She spoke.

He knelt and looked at the markers at the scene. "Do you have pictures of the symbol carvings on each of the bodies?"

"I do." She replied.

The sheriff walked up and joined them. "Good morning, Agent Porter."

"Morning, Sheriff," Porter said.

Madison handed him five photos of the carvings. He inspected each, then handed them back to her.

"They're occult symbols," he said.

"I know. The rest of the team thought so," she replied.

The sheriff pulled out his cigarettes and a lighter. He lit one up and exhaled the smoke into the crisp morning air.

"And what do you think?" Agent Porter asked.

"I think the killer is from out of town," the sheriff said.

"Could you be a little more specific?" Porter asked.

The sheriff adjusted his hat. "I don't want to go on record as saying who the killer is until I have more evidence or more proof."

"Of course, sheriff. I'm more interested in your opinion."

The sheriff smoked his cigarette and then turned to face Porter. "I think it's that crazy son of a bitch from Hawthorn."

Sounding shocked, Agent Porter asked. "Robert Owens?"

"That's the one."

"He's the brother of the first victim."

"Yes, I know. I've been monitoring him. Since his sister's death, he's been in and out of the hospital with a variety of mental illnesses. He just was placed back in for a violent assault on an elderly woman. He is one angry man." The sheriff said.

"Where's Owens now?" Porter asked.

The sheriff put his hands on his hips. "He's locked up at Hawthorn Memorial."

"Is there any way we can talk to him?" Porter asked.

"No, he's in the psych ward. He's not allowed visitors."

Porter walked closer to the sheriff. "I need to talk to him."

"We can't do anything official. I shouldn't have told you anything. I shouldn't have even admitted to you that the sheriff's department had been monitoring him."

"It's ok. I understand."

"You can talk to him off the record. There is one problem, though." The sheriff sighed.

"What?" Porter asked.

"He's been sort of silent since his sister's death. He hasn't spoken a word. Not one fucking word."

Circling around the scene, Porter insisted. "That's fine. I'll talk to him."

"How are you going to do that?"

"I'll think of something."

The sheriff finished his cigarette and flicked the butt onto the ground. He watched as the smoke drifted into the sky and disappeared.

"Alright, I'll talk to the hospital and see if we can't get you in to see him."

The sheriff walked over to his car and pulled out his phone. The FBI profiler watched him as he walked up to a couple of his deputies and talked to them.

"What do you think?" Porter asked Madison.

"I don't know. The idea is interesting, but the evidence doesn't match up."

"What do you mean?"

"The mutilations, the bite marks, the blood being drained, and the symbols. It's just all so damn weird." She spoke.

"That's why I'm here, to give you some answers."

"Do you have any ideas that we can go on?" she asked.

"No, not yet, but I will."

"I hope so."

"We should go. I need to make some phone calls."

Madison and Porter walked back to his car. He set his briefcase in the backseat and then he got in.

"Nice to meet you, Deputy. I'll be in touch in a day or so."

"I look forward to working with you."

He got into his car and started the engine. Madison watched as he drove off into the distance.

She could not stop thinking about the case. Anyone would have thought it was a waste of time. There were so many better people to come in and help them.

Madison went back to the station and sat down at her desk.

What did he know about their small town?

He was an occult expert, but he had no experience with cases like this.

Madison pulled up her files on Robert Owens. He had been a suspect once before. Back then, they had written him up as a crank. Now nothing that he said was false, or even that outlandish. He had a close connection to the family, and he was crazy, but did that make him a serial killer?

Not according to the evidence.

Madison walked over to the computer. She typed Robert Owens into Google and waited.

A list of results appeared on the screen. The first link took her to a blog post.

This entry was posted on October 11, 2021, at 12:00 AM and tagged with Facial Recognition and privacy.

She clicked on the post, and another link appeared at the bottom of the blog.

The top of the blog post featured a picture of a man: he was a tall, muscular man with graying hair. He had an unkempt beard that was dusted with white, licking his neck and the lower half of his face. His eyes were sunken and dark, like those of an old dog that had seen too much death. He wore a white T-shirt and leather restraints around his wrists and ankles.

A brown bar above his head held a tag reading "Robert Owens."

Madison clicked on the link, and another tab opened in her browser to show his medical history.

He had been committed to the psych ward after a violent outburst. Acting irrationally, he had attacked another patient in the ward with a fork.

Looks like he got locked up before our latest body was found, she thought to herself.

That meant he could not be their killer.

"Damn it," Madison said aloud.

She opened another browser window and clicked on the link for the psych ward at Hawthorn Memorial. She pulled up Robert Owens' medical file and read his history.

The file had been marked with a red stamp: "**DO NOT DISCHARGE - LIFE THREATENING PROBLEM.**"

There was a bearded young man who walked into the hospital in a straitjacket. He was tall and gaunt, with sunken eyes and a nose that had been broken many times in the past. His beard was unkempt as if he had scratched his face until his skin was raw. He had a malicious look, an evil smirk that lingered on his face.

Closing her laptop, she stood up and exhaled a long breath.

"How could I be so stupid?" She asked herself.

She walked over to the sheriff's office and knocked on the door.

"Come in," the sheriff said.

"I want to talk to you about Robert Owens," Madison said.

"I told you I'd get you in to see him."

"That's not why I'm here."

"Then what's the problem? Isn't he, our killer?"

"No, he's not."

"Are you sure?"

"Yes."

"How can you be so sure?"

"He's been locked up in the psych ward since they found the body. They haven't released him."

Leaning back in his chair, the sheriff exhaled a long breath.

"Fine, but I think we should keep an eye on him, anyway."

"I agree."

Madison turned to leave and then walked towards the door. She pulled it open and left the sheriff's office.

She had a ton of information on the murders and the symbols.

The ding of her phone interrupted her thoughts. She picked it up and answered.

"Hello?"

"Hey Madison, this is agent Porter. Do you have time to get together tonight? I have a few things about the case that we should talk about."

"How about now?"

"I'm at a bar. Across the street from the hotel."

"I'll see you there in ten minutes."

Grabbing her keys, putting her gun in its holster, and locking the door, Madison left her apartment. In the cool morning, she jogged the two blocks to the bar and opened the door. She paused at the threshold and let her eyes adjust to the darkness. When they did, she saw agent Porter sitting at the bar. He had a beer in one hand and a folder in the other.

"Hey," he said.

"Hey," she replied.

She sat down on a bar stool and ordered a beer, a long draft. The bartender quickly brought her a drink, and she took a long swig as she looked around the bar.

It was a dive. The floors were smudged with dirt and the tables sticky, and the music was loud. A group of people was crammed into the corner playing darts. The bartender served the beer in a clean glass and the smell of cigarette smoke filled the air.

"This place is a dump," Madison said.

"I know, but so far, it's my favorite bar in town."

"When I think of a bar, I think of a classy place." She laughed.

"I'm not classy," he replied.

She didn't respond; she just sipped her beer.

"I want you to tell me about your thoughts on the case," Madison said.

"Sure. I can tell you what I have found out so far, but I know that you want more than that." He answered.

Putting down her beer, she asked. "I want to know your suspect profile."

"Of course. I've profiled hundreds of people for the FBI. This is nothing new to me."

"Has the sheriff told you his theory yet?" she asked.

"Yes, and he's been eyeing me with a strange look on his face." He chuckled.

"He thinks that it's Robert Owens." She stated.

Madison shifted in her seat and leaned toward him. "It isn't him. He was locked up during the last murder."

"That's what I saw when I looked him up." He spoke.

"Whatever. What is your profile?" She asked.

141

"It's a young man, maybe a teenager, or early 20s. He is a loner, with no girlfriend, maybe no friends at all. He's probably a virgin, and he's a very private person. He's smart, but he's not athletic. He's more comfortable in his head than in reality. He can't handle confrontation, so he's probably submissive. He's probably religious."

Madison looked shocked. "A religious serial killer? That makes little sense."

"That's what I said at first. It would certainly give him his guilt." He spoke.

Madison took another long drink of her beer and then slammed the empty glass on the bar. She waved at the bartender and ordered another beer.

"So, you think that he's punishing them for having sex?" she asked.

"That's the thing. I don't think he's punishing them. I think he's punishing himself."

"Why?" she whispered.

Twirling his glass on the bar. "I think he's delusional. He believes that he is doing something for the greater good. He thinks that he's doing god's will, and he's going to rid the world of sinners."

"So, you think he's a martyr?" she asked.

"Not exactly. I think he is a jilted lover, who's also religious. He's lost his girlfriend to someone, maybe another man, but he can't handle the guilt. So, he punishes himself as well as everyone else."

" A crime of passion?"

"More like a crime of lust."

She looked shocked. "Even the men he killed?"

"Even them. He hates himself for his gay thoughts, but he also hates the people who committed a sin."

"Sounds pretty nutty."

Looking down at his glass, he said. "It's pretty common. I've seen it a lot."

She leaned into him. "What do you think his next step is?"

"I don't know. He is escalating the violence and the frequency of the murders. I think he's going to continue for a while."

"Like how long?" she asked.

"Weeks, months. Maybe longer."

"I hope you're wrong." She announced.

"So do I."

Madison finished her beer. She was not a big drinker, so two beers made her tipsy. Walking back to her apartment, it lost her in thought. The killer was nothing like they thought he would be. He did not fit their profile at all. She stumbled on a crack in the sidewalk and laughed as she righted herself. The moon's glow seeped through leaves and cast a dim light on the way home.

"Maybe I'm wrong," she said to herself.

When she got back to her place, she went to her room. She removed her shoes, set her gun down next to her phone, and then sat on the edge of the bed. Taking a long breath, she let it out as she closed her eyes for a moment.

"What a fucked-up case."

Brushing her hair, she examined her face in the mirror. It was a face she no longer recognized. There were circles under her eyes, and her face was pale. She looked as if she had stopped aging at thirty and then suddenly started aging again. The wrinkles around her mouth betrayed a woman who had lived too long. Dark circles underscored her eyes, and if you poked at one of the thin lines on her face, it would turn into a crevice. She looked as if only another few decades would erase the tautness of youth from her skin and age her to death. She looked as if she hadn't slept since graduating high school or making love with the boy she knew back then.

She stood up and grabbed the water glass on the side of her bed. The ice inside was long melted. She took a long drink of warm water. She did not like to drink much when she went to sleep, and this warm water was all she had wanted. Her thoughts were confusing her when she went to the bathroom.

The room was spinning, and it felt like the world she had left behind had passed for a new one, which she could not recognize because she'd never been in it before. She sat down hard on the toilet seat and pulled her knees up to her chin. She had too much to drink to sleep, so she got undressed and took a long shower. The hot water beat down on her head, pounding on her skull, but it was better than looking at anything else.

She did not know how long she stood there, but eventually; she turned the water off. Wrapping herself in a towel, she stepped out of the shower. With a sigh, she made her way to bed and crawled in.

144

Sitting on her bed, Madison held her cell phone out in front of her. She picked it up and considered throwing it across the room. She did not know what to do with it, so she dropped it to the floor. The sound of the cell phone hitting the floor filled the room, making Madison jump.

"Fuck."

Just sitting there, doing nothing. That is how the day went, and that is how the night went. She was awake all night and didn't get any sleep at all.

She almost called in sick, but she knew it wouldn't do any good. Even if she didn't go in, the man would continue killing. There was nothing she could do, and she had to accept the fact that this case was bigger than her. She stared at the ceiling with her phone in front of her face. In the screen's light, she saw a bug crawl across the ground and flip over onto its back. There, it struggled to right itself and continued its crawl across the floor.

She stood and walked to the balcony of her apartment. She was afraid to climb over the railing, but she knew that her fear was irrational. History and statistics were on her side. She could overcome her fear of heights, she knew, and she could look down to the ground below. If she fell, she would die. Her death would be the end of her story and nothing more. The moments after her death were like a hole at the center of a circle. They would fill the hole with memories of people who loved her and the life she had lived and dreamed of, but it would remain empty. The life she lived, played like a movie at the center of her mind, a movie about a woman who had filled every moment of her life with as much as she could, who had chosen love over fear many times and helped others do the same.

"What am I going to do?"

She had too much on her plate. Putting her uniform on that smelled like beer and cigarettes, she grabbed her gun and went outside. The mist of the day covered the base of the trees and filtered through the floorboards of the porch. Frosty grass crunched underfoot.

The tiny car drifted out of the parking lot, and she drove on autopilot to the sheriff's office.

Driving on autopilot was unlike her. She was always in control, and she was always aware of her surroundings. But today her mind was full of nothing.

"What's wrong with me?"

Closing the door behind her, Madison sat down at the desk. She looked over at the sheriff, who was sitting at his desk, reading the paper. He set aside his donut and folded up the paper, giving her a nod. She nodded back and then sat down.

The air in the police station was cool and crisp, just as she liked it. Madison wrapped her scarf around her neck as she stared at her partner's empty desk. With a sigh, she waited for the day to start.

She flipped up the collar on her coat and hoisted a large pack over her shoulder. The weight of it made her grunt slightly, but she ignored the pain and went on. She clutched a cup of steaming coffee in one hand, the steam curling into her face to warm her. The sun was just rising, painting a golden glow of warmth over the horizon. Through the open window a barn owl hooted as it flew overhead, swooping through the trees as if on patrol. She stopped for a second to look back at her vehicle; it looked like a tiny toy in this vast land.

"Hey," she said with a grin. The sheriff returned the smile. "Sleep well?"

"Like a baby."

"Good."

"Did agent Porter have any luck with the victim's phone?"

"No. It's still tracking."

"Shit. Anything else?"

"Nothing, we're still waiting for the techs."

"What about the surveillance video?"

"They're working on it."

"Well, let's get to it."

Madison wiped the small beads of sweat forming on her brow with the back of her hand, then stood up from her desk and followed the sheriff's large silhouette out to his car. The sun was bright and high in the sky, and there were a few clouds floating around. A bright, beautiful day for investigating a murder.

Their first stop was the victim's house, an old wood cabin that sat in a dell of trees. The overgrown lawn was choked with weeds and grasses, and the shutters hung on their hinges like old teeth. The sheriff got out of his truck and shouted something at Madison, but she could not hear him through the window. He got back into his truck, revved the engine, and drove up a dirt path that cut through a stand of pine trees about half a mile from the mill.

Pinecones snapped under the tires as they drove deeper into the forest, swerving around puddles of leaves almost big enough to swallow them whole. The windows were all fogged, so Madison couldn't see out, but she could feel the chilly breeze on her face and heavy drops of rain on her skin, forming on their exhalation and dripping down in front of her, tracing trails in the fog. She saw the long, spindly branches of pine trees reaching up to the sky and whipping loudly against the flanks of their truck. The scene reminded her of when she had driven out here with her mother and sister. Amid swirling winds and a backdrop of black stretching sky and treetops morphing into a forest of varying shades of dark browns and blacks, there was a silence that filled her ears, deafening in its intensity. The raindrops froze and fell through the air slowly, but at a quickening rate until they plummeted downward in an explosion on all sides, crashing against the ground like hail bullets. Nothing moved out there but Madison's own breath.

They stepped out and saw the techs going in and out of the house. The last one closed the door behind him before he stepped off the porch. As the sheriff and Madison approached, a few turned to look around. Two men leaned against a car. Each of them was holding a triple-shot espresso in their hands like it was a grenade about to go off.

"What is it?" one of them asked.

They walked under a tree with fat needles that hung over their heads like a canopy. The sheriff put his hands up to ward off the needles. When he and Madison reached the bottom of the steps, he bent over and dropped his hand to the side, and she rushed forward to steady him.

"What were you doing this morning?" the sheriff asked, "Pulling the needles from your fat ass?"

The tech said nothing.

"This is where he lived? Good God, what the fuck did he do for fun in this place?"

"Whatever you got to do, I guess." the tech said with a chuckle.

"What a place to live. Does it look like he was killed here? I don't see any blood."

"No, he wasn't killed here," the tech said. "It was somewhere else."

"And you know this because?"

"There's no blood. There are no signs of a struggle."

Walking closer to the tech, she asked. "So, he just went with the murderer. Is that what you're saying?"

"I don't know."

"Well, what makes you think he was taken somewhere else to be killed?"

"Because there's no sign of a struggle. See these bushes? They haven't been disturbed." he answered.

The tech pointed toward a cluster of bushes; the leaves were a rich, glossy green and curled from the cold and the branches drooped like jolly green giants.

"That means there was no struggle?"

"And see here. This is the door to the shed. It's locked. It doesn't look like anyone has been in or out for a while. If there was a struggle, the door would be open."

"So, you're saying that he went with the murderer willingly?"

"Maybe."

"And you know this because of the door?" she asked, raising her voice.

"In part, yeah."

"You're one strange little shit, you know that?"

"It's what makes me good at my job," he said sarcastically.

"Yeah, well, strange is all we have on this thing. Anything else?"

"No, that's about it."

"Well, keep at it, and let me know if you find anything."

"Will do."

A drone hovered over the trees, and Madison watched it. They pointed the camera down at the ground, some sort of heat sensor scanning the area. After it was done, it moved off in another direction.

"If you don't mind my asking, what's with the drone?" Madison asked.

"Good question. We got a request from the feds to use it last night. They're collaborating with us on this case, and they want to make sure they turn up everything they can."

"Well, good luck with that," Madison said.

"God. What a place to live," the sheriff repeated.

"You don't know the half of it."

"No, I guess I don't."

The sheriff went back to his truck, and Madison followed. After sitting down, he turned the key in the ignition and the truck roared to life. The engine chugged, sticking and stalling as it tried to pick up speed. He kicked it again, and the engine coughed out a huge puff of steam from its blackened and rotten guts.

"Cold," he said. "You ready to go?"

"Yeah."

"Then let's go."

Madison climbed into the passenger side and slammed the door shut. Sheriff Cross started the engine and pulled away from the curb. The car rolled down Muir Lane, swerving slightly to avoid large piles of dog shit that dotted the street but only by inches. Madison did not mind. She knew life was like this: random, dangerous, and full of shit that you must accept and deal with. The car zoomed onto the main road and passed through a series of side roads, each meant to loop back to the main road eventually. Soon, they reached the mill. It was near to where they were. Only a few more turns would lead them back home. The road went through the trees and through a cluster of old houses that did not look any better than the shack in the woods.

They continued back to the station in silence. It was only a few minutes away, but it felt like hours. Madison said nothing, and the sheriff was silent. They were both thinking about how easy it would be for someone to take a life. It would only take a few minutes, and when it was done, there would be no trace of what happened. No trace of a struggle, no trace of murder, nothing. They would just be gone, and no one would ever know what happened.

All it took was a few minutes, and then another minute to get rid of the body, two more minutes to make sure there was no trace of what was done, and then another minute. It was easy; it took extraordinarily little time, and it was final.

The sheriff pulled into the station, and they both got out. They walked into the station; the sheriff making small talk, but his words were just words, and Madison was only listening to the sound of his voice, not the actual words coming out of his mouth. Both were tired. They had been doing this for hours and the only thing they had to show for it was a dusty gray trailer, a pile of pine needles, and a word: maybe.

Now they were thinking about the same thing, but neither one of them would admit it. They were looking for evidence, looking for something that would lead them to the killer, and instead, they found nothing but a pile of dirt, a house, and a body.

The sun was setting, and its last glow fell across their office windows. They walked into the building and sat down. The air was cool, and the sun was warm. The sky was blue, but it would not last. Soon the sky would be black, the air would be cool, and the sun would be gone. It would leave them to wander in the dark.

THIRTEEN

At school, Jenny could not concentrate, much less keep her eyes open. She tried to keep up with her work, but she could not.

The teacher was late, and the class went to lunch early because of it. They were outside, in the sun, and Jenny sat down at the picnic table and gazed around. There were a few people here and there and a few more lazing around in the forest. There were not many people, and it was quiet. The weather was cooling off.

Her mind was racing around with thoughts of Leon.

She could still visualize his kind smile and could still feel his hand in hers. She could still hear him ask her to dance. She could still feel his hand on her back, guiding her to the center of the dance floor. She could still smell his cologne, still see the glint in his eye, still taste the brush of his lips against hers. She could still feel him against her and see him smile at her and hear him tell her how much he loved her. He was so funny, so smart, so handsome, so kind, and so loving. The glint in his eyes had said it all: she was so beautiful, and he was so lucky.

After lunch, she went to her next class. She wanted to avoid Dana and the popular crowd. They gossiped and churned out vicious rumors during class and ate in the cafeteria. She could not stand it any longer. Did Dana think she was still with Leon? What would Dana think if she knew that Jenny and Leon had slept together? What would she think if she knew Jenny had fallen in love with a guy who lived in a big house and who was an artist?

Just then, Dana walked into the classroom, laughing with a friend. It tinged her laughter with joy and excitement, and her eyes were bright with fun. She scanned Jenny's face, and an uncertain smile lifted the corners of her mouth. Jenny smiled back. Had Dana been waiting for her? Had she noticed Jenny finally? Lately, Dana had been so busy with her new friends, she did not seem to care much about Jenny or what she did. That was because she was having so much fun now! Jenny should tell her she was going out with Leon. It might make her happy.

But what if Dana did not understand? What if she got angry and jealous? What if Leon got angry, too?

She tried to make eye contact with Dana, but it was hopeless. Dana was so busy talking with her friends that she did not even notice Jenny. Instead, Jenny pulled out her cell phone and started texting Leon.

"Are you free tonight?"

And she waited.

Two minutes later he wrote: "I'd love to hang out."

She wrote: "Great."

"Where?"

"I don't know."

"I don't know either."

She looked at Dana's long, tan, smooth legs. The tight jeans and high-heeled boots. She looked at Dana's waist and the straight, perfect, narrow waist. Her sultry hip with the tight jeans. The perfect, firm ass.

She imagined Leon kissing those legs and licking her skin. She imagined Leon kissing the small of her back and biting the skin above her waist.

"Jenny? Jenny?"

She snapped back to reality.

"Jenny, pay attention, please."

"Yes, Ms. Hale. Sorry, Ms. Hale."

Jenny's mind was racing. All she could think about was Leon.

The bell rang. It jarred Jenny from her deep thoughts. As she headed out the door, she pulled her phone from her pocket and slipped it into her backpack. She slipped the zipper closed over her phone and pulled the front of her hoodie over it. She ran out the door and headed to the corner. Maybe if she walked fast, she would get there before he left. Maybe if she could just talk to him alone, he would understand!

She felt a hand on her shoulder.

"Hey, Jenny."

She looked up to see Charlotte.

"You look like you're heading to a funeral."

She smiled and laughed. "What's up with you?"

She walked away, and Jenny followed close behind.

"I mean, it's Wednesday," Charlotte said. "We might as well be out of school in a few days."

"What's the big deal?" Jenny did not respond.

"Something wrong?" Charlotte asked.

Jenny saw Dana. She was on her cell phone, walking away from them.

"No, I'm fine," Jenny said.

"Why are you acting so weird?" Charlotte asked.

"Dude lay off me," Jenny said.

"Fine, suit yourself."

Charlotte turned from her and walked off.

That evening when she was home from work, Jenny sat in her room, listening to music. She was dressed in a long, sleeveless black dress. She liked to wear something a little sexier when she went out. It was silk, and it fell below her knees. It fit her well, but it also showed off all her curves. Her heels tapped out a slow, steady, melancholy beat on the carpeted floor. A few moments later, there was a loud knock on the door. Tripping over her feet, she ran out to answer the door. Peering through the peephole, she saw it was Charlotte, Meg, and Dana. Charlotte was holding a bottle of wine and Meg was holding a bag of chips.

Charlotte knocked again and said, "I know you're there, Jenny. I saw your car. Open the door."

She opened the door.

"Hey," Charlotte said.

"Hey yourself," Meg said. "Come on, Jenny, we just want to talk."

"C'mon in," she said.

Jenny opened her door.

As soon as the door was open, Charlotte burst in, followed by Meg. Dana was the last to enter the room. Dana looked at Jenny. The door shut behind Dana.

"What's up?" Dana said.

"Why didn't you tell me?" Charlotte said.

"Tell you what?"

"You know what!"

"What are you talking about? You're crazy!"

"I saw you," Charlotte said. "I saw you with him. I saw you with Leon, and you didn't even tell me about it!"

"Oh," Jenny said. "That."

"What?" Dana said. "What are you talking about?"

Charlotte stopped abruptly, as though a physical barrier had appeared before her. The surrounding air became charged with a single word that Dana could not identify. It hung in the air like a tangible thing - a corpse hanging in space - but it had no form and no meaning. She knew she should feel something, but she did not know what it was.

"I saw her with him," Charlotte said, "and I'm sorry I didn't tell you, but I thought you were with him, and I didn't want to say anything."

"What are you talking about?" Dana said.

Dana moved forward, her hand still on the doorknob of the trailer, and at that moment, she knew exactly what Charlotte was talking about. Exactly what Charlotte was referring to. She turned to face her friend, who was still staring at the ground.

Coming out of his room wearing headphones, Jenny's brother Joey saw the four girls standing in the hallway. He was dressed in an army jacket, a black t-shirt that had

Ramones across the front, and a pair of jeans. He stopped walking and looked at Meg, who had her blonde hair pulled back and wore a sweet, girly smile. Then he looked at Dana with her bright eyes and blonde hair, who was dressed much more modestly in a light-blue shirt that matched her eyes. His gaze lingered for a minute on Charlotte before looking down at his feet and pushing his wavy brown hair from his brow. He walked up to Jenny and hugged her, wrapping his arms around her shoulders, then he hugged Charlotte and gave her a kiss on the cheek. Then he looked at Dana with her bright eyes.

"Hey," he said, "your friends came here."

"Ya, why don't you go back to your room?" Jenny told him.

"Okay," he said and walked back to his room.

After the door shut, Jenny said, "I'm so sorry. I'm so sorry."

The girls looked at Jenny.

"I'm sorry. I didn't mean for you to find out this way," Jenny said.

Charlotte looked at her and said, "Oh, so you're just sorry that we found out?"

"No, I'm sorry that I didn't tell you, or at least warn you before you guys came here. I'm sorry that I made a fool of myself in front of you."

"A fool of yourself?" Charlotte said.

"Yes," Jenny said.

"What's going on?" asked Dana.

"Leon asked me out," Jenny said. "I didn't tell you because I didn't know how to, and I didn't know how to tell you because I was afraid that if I said something, you would try to stop me from going."

"How could you not tell us?" Charlotte said.

"I don't know. I just waited for you to say something, and I tried to talk to you about it, and you never did."

Charlotte was silent, and Dana said, "Well, aren't you going to tell us that you're going out with him?"

"I am going out with him."

"Wait a second," Charlotte said. "What, are you two dating?"

"No," Jenny said.

"So, you're not going out with him?" asked Dana.

"No," Jenny said.

Dana looked at Charlotte, who was looking at the floor.

Jenny said, "I'm sorry. I don't know what to say. It's just that we're going out one time. We are just going to have one date and then that's it."

Charlotte looked at Jenny and said, "You're going on a date with Dana's boyfriend?"

"He's not her boyfriend," Jenny said.

"You're still going on a date with him," Charlotte said.

"Yes, I'm sorry."

"Good," Charlotte said. "At least you're not dating him."

"I'm sorry," Jenny repeated.

"We should go," said Charlotte. "I have to get to the grocery store."

"Wait," Jenny said. "Let me explain to you why this is happening, at least for me."

"Explain...?" said Charlotte.

"Yes, explain," said Dana.

"Okay, I've never felt like this before. I've never felt so strongly about someone so quickly. But it's not like that for me. I don't fall in love with someone. I don't get attached to someone. I don't know what happened, alright? I don't know why this is happening to me, but it is. And I'm sorry if I'm hurting you, Dana, but I can't help it. This is just how I feel. I didn't plan for it to happen to me, but it did, and I can't help it, I just feel... I just feel like I'm falling in love."

The intensity in Dana's eyes was clear as she stepped forward, her long, flowing scarf trailing behind her.

"Hey, no problem, we will always be best friends, Jenny," she said. "We were going to go to the park tonight and party, your lover boy Leon is going to be there."

"I guess, I just need to tell my brother what's going on... hold on a second," Jenny said.

Jenny walked back to her brother's door and looked inside. The room was cramped, with one bed and a small television set. She could hear her brother's video game in the next room, which he had turned up so loudly that he could not possibly hear anything else. Jenny knocked on the door to get his attention.

"Hey, I'm going out tonight," Jenny said.

"Okay," Joey replied.

"I'll be back late, and honestly, I don't know how late. Dad's coming home from work in a couple of hours."

"Okay," Joey said again, his eyes still trained to his video game.

"I'm sorry. I wish I could spend some time with you tonight, but I didn't even know that I was going out until just a little bit ago. I know it's really sudden, but I promise I'll make it up to you another night."

"Alright, have fun," said Joey, his voice monotonous.

"Thanks, Joey," Jenny said.

She walked back to her friends, who were standing exactly where she had left them.

"Alright, let's go," she said.

Jenny fingered her keys and smiled at Dana. "It's great to hang out with you," she said. Dana shuffled her feet and looked down at the ground.

"Yeah, sure," she replied.

Jenny reached out and patted Dana's shoulder. "Let's head out the door," she said.

Dana and Jenny locked arms and when they got outside of the trailer, Dana said, "Jump in the car!"

The car was pearly white with a red stripe down the side. The seats were black leather and had red piping around them that matched the knee-high red heels Charlotte wore. She sat in the backseat and put on her seatbelt. Dana started up the car and backed out of the space.

The park was two miles away from Jenny's trailer and was part of a heavily wooded state park. It was a big playground that had a few hills, two basketball courts, a baseball diamond, and a small lake. It looked like a colorful painting of movement and bodies. There were teenagers everywhere. The girls piled out of the car. The landscape was a blur of green, streaming past the windows.

Their other friend, Rachel, was standing behind the car. The girls were sitting in the backseat and could not see her yet.

Rachel's boyfriend, Donny, who was tall and had soft, light brown hair and blue eyes, ran up to her. She squealed when he lifted her up and swung her around.

"Babe!" Donny shouted as he spun through the air with Rachel in his arms. She felt as if she were flying, like a bird released from a cage into a wild, untamed field of flowers. She felt airy.

"Hi, guys!" Rachel's voice called.

"Rachel?" Dana said.

"Yeah, I'm surprised you guys didn't see me," Rachel said.

"We can't really see anything because we're in the back-seat," Dana said.

"Does anybody have any weed? I really need some," Rachel said.

"Oh, of course, you're going to ask me," Dana said. "I just got here, so no, I don't have any yet."

"My mouth is watering," Rachel said. "I haven't eaten anything all day. I just want a snack."

"Well, we don't have long to wait," Dana said. "Just hang in there, will you? My stomach is growling, too."

"You two are so pathetic. Why don't you get something to eat?" Charlotte said.

"We'll have to go to the gas station because I don't have any cash," Dana said.

"I'll drive," Charlotte said.

"Thanks," Dana said.

"Dude, what is your problem?" asked Charlotte.

"Oh," said Rachel. "I'm sorry, I forgot to introduce you to my boyfriend, Donny,"

"Hi Donny," Charlotte, Dana, and Jenny greeted.

The girls walked into the gas station and began getting food. Rachel got a burrito, a large drink, and some fries; Charlotte got a sandwich, some chips, and a drink; and

Dana got french fries and a milkshake. Jenny got a bag of chips and a soda. The girls frowned at the people living in the RV across from the gas station. They wanted to get their food and go back van where the comforts of home awaited them.

"I like your shoes," Rachel told Dana. "They're really cute. Are those Christian Louboutin heels?"

"Yeah," Dana said.

"Are they real?" asked Rachel.

"Yes," said Dana.

"Oh my God, I wish I had shoes like that," Rachel said.

"Here," Dana said. "Take them."

She took off her shoes and handed them to Rachel. Rachel took them.

"Yeah, they're kind of big on me," she said.

"Do they fit you?" Dana asked.

"Yeah!" Rachel exclaimed. "I love them. Thank you so much. I'll pay you back for them."

"You don't have to."

"You should have seen her face when she saw them," Charlotte said.

"I know," Dana said.

"I can't believe you just gave them to me," said Rachel.

"They looked good on you," Dana said.

"Aw, that was so sweet of you," Rachel said.

"No problem," Dana said.

Walking back to the park, Meg and Jake joined them. Jake's hair was so black and full that it spilled out from beneath the edges of the red t-shirt with a black skull on it. This completed his look, which was casual and fun, like everything else about him. The two had met at a Halloween party a few years before, and he had been so witty and charming that she could not help but take to him.

All Jenny could do was think about Leon and when he would show up. The girls walked over to the large metal slide. Rachel took off Dana's heels and put them on Charlotte. Charlotte tried to kick off her sandals, and it was difficult. She had to really struggle to pull them off. Blue, yellow, and green lights lit up the sky in a shimmering display of light. Some kids were singing and playing guitar, while others were trying to smoke cigarettes or joints. Jenny felt like she was in a movie, like a scene from a romantic comedy. Rachel had already eaten her food and was now throwing the wrapper into a trash can. She then bounced over to Jenny and grabbed her arm, squeezing it tightly.

"Will you come down the slide with me?" Rachel asked.

"Of course," replied Jenny.

The two girls climbed up the stairs and sat on the top of the slide. They made their way down the slide. It was exhilarating. They got to the bottom of the slide and climbed back up the stairs and did it again, laughing and giggling all the way down. Some were playing an informal game of baseball with a tennis ball and a bat. Jenny could not help but laugh at the guys who had to chase the ball down after they hit it. Donny and Jake were standing off to the side, talking. Dana was sitting in a green plastic chair, looking down at her feet. Charlotte had wandered off a few minutes before, to talk to some guys who were playing guitar.

Rachel and Jenny climbed up the stairs again and slid down the slide.

Jenny thought she saw somebody approaching the park from the woods. She strained her eyes to see who it was.

"Do you see that?" Jenny said.

"What?" asked Rachel.

"I see somebody coming out of the woods," Jenny said.

"Who is it?" asked Rachel.

"I don't know," said Jenny, squinting.

She increased the speed of her slide down, keeping her eyes fixed on the woods. A small grove of trees and bushes that provided some privacy surrounded the slide. She heard the footsteps before she saw the person coming toward her, and then a shadowy figure appeared. Her heart did a tiny flip when she saw it was Leon. It was Leon! He sauntered over to her and offered his hand. She took it, and he pulled her close with one strong motion. She bent over, placing her hands on her knees as she gasped for air and laughed.

"Hi," Leon said. He was dressed in all black and wearing a hoodie, with his glasses pulled low over his nose.

"Oh my God, Leon!" Jenny exclaimed.

"What?" asked Leon.

"Oh my God, I am so happy to see you," Jenny said.

Jenny and Leon held hands as they walked down the red plastic slide. They slung their legs over the side, Jenny on the left, Leon on the right, and sat in the green plastic chairs. Dana was smoking a cigarette and talking to Jake. She blew smoke rings into the air and watched them float away. Jake pushed his finger into a paper cup and made a hole in it. He poured some soda into it and took a big drink. Jenny looked at him as though he were crazy. Dana pushed her dark hair out of her eyes, gave Jenny an understanding smile, and took another puff of her cigarette. The smoke smelled like a campfire smoldering in the cool autumn air, like hot chocolate with just the right number of marshmallows dissolved in it, like a spring morning after a rainstorm.

Two girls walked over and sat down on the grass. They smiled at the guitarists and started talking. The guys strummed their guitars and sang a song, while the girls giggled and touched their arms. Jenny sat down in her chair next to Leon.

"Want to take a walk with me? I have something that I need to tell you... show you," Leon said.

"All right," Jenny replied.

Leon held Jenny's small hand in his large hand and led her across the muddy, uneven ground to a secluded area of the park. They had to walk in single file to avoid the waist-high grass and the trees that blocked out the light, hiding them from the rest of the park. The trees rustled in the wind, and high in the branches, Jenny could see a small bird flitting from one branch to another. They walked into the woods, still holding hands. The trees blocked out the light and sheltered them from the rest of the park. It was cool inside the forest, with long shadows painted across the ground by the moonlight filtering through the treetops.

The music and the voices from the park died down, and the sounds of traffic from the highway were soon muffled.

The woods were black. Leon stopped walking. Turning around to face Jenny, he stood close to her. He then knelt on the grass. He wondered if Jenny would like the gift he was about to give her. It was a gift that was incredibly special and important to him, and it meant the world to him that she be the one to have it. She leaned her head into his hand and closed her eyes. He put his hand on the back of her head and pulled her close to him. She kissed him, and there was that same feeling that he felt the first time they kissed.

"So, what did you want to show me?" asked Jenny.

The branches of the trees shifted slightly and a young woman with blonde hair stepped out with a young man. Her red dress shimmered in the soft moonlight, and her friend had a glint of mischief in his eyes. She looked at him, her expression dreamy and sweet, and he looked back at her, his lips slightly parted. He took a step towards her before running across the meadow towards Jenny.

"You are Jenny," said the woman.

"She isn't ready," said Leon, stepping in front of Jenny. "Leave now."

"Ah Leon, is she the one that you spoke so highly of?" said the woman.

"Get away from her. I won't tell you again," Leon said.

The woman's eyes turned from a clear, bright blue to a dark black, and her face became expressionless. She grabbed Leon's arm and pulled him closer to her.

167

"We do not need another to join us, Leon. We need to feed."

The woman's pupils dilated to the size of two large quarters and her top eyelids drooped down to cover her eyes. Her teeth grew long and jagged and her mouth stretched open wide as she hissed.

Leon's head jerked back, and his eyes rolled back in his head. The woman's black eyes flashed with a purple light and Leon's mouth opened and closed.

Jenny was frozen in her tracks, her heart racing so fast she was trembling.

"What have you done with him?" asked Jenny. She stumbled backwards in fear.

Three more people walked out of the woods and stood next to Jenny and Leon. The two with her were tall and muscular, wearing jeans, and hoodies, and had their hair in ponytails. The other person was a tall, skinny boy with a bag over his shoulder. He wore a polo shirt and baseball hat. He was far away enough that she couldn't see the color of his eyes, but she could see that they were looking right at her.

The two people next to her stepped toward her, and the air became thick with tension. She heard rushing wind next to her, and she saw the flash of light.

The moon turned red, and two birds spiraled to the ground. Jenny froze. Something was staring back at her. It had no face, just a black silhouette, and it was staring at her.

"Jenny, I am not like the others," Leon said. He turned around and faced the shadow that was standing behind him. Jenny saw it was a man, but there were just glowing red eyes, no nose, no mouth, no ears, just a black silhouette.

"We are hungry now, Leon!" it spoke. "We have given you so much in return for so little. Why deny us?"

"I need to protect Jenny; she can be one of us," said Leon.

"We need to feed Leon!" said the figure.

Tears ran down Leon's eyes, and his knees shook.

"We need to feed!" said the figure.

Jenny saw Leon's legs buckle, and he fell to the ground.

Jenny gasped, but the air was knocked from her as two powerful hands grabbed her from behind and pulled her into the darkness. Her feet kicked to get a foothold on the ground. She groped for a rock or stick or anything she could defend herself with, but there was nothing. A voice swelled within her, and she shrieked through the darkness. "No! No! No! No! No!"

A low, guttural growl arose from the very belly of the blackness. It swirled, forming a dense mist, and then the bottom dropped out of the fog, and it fell to the ground. A fast-moving shadow ran toward Jenny. A silhouette emerged from the darkness. She could hear it breathing. The blackness melted off the beast and its true form became clear. It rose from the ground and stood on its hind legs, opening its mouth to reveal crooked teeth and a long, wet, pink tongue. The beast's yellow eyes locked onto Jenny's. Jenny felt a rush of emotions: fear, anger, desperation, longing to be dead.

"No!" Leon shouted.

Another beast walked in front of him covered in dark brown matted fur that seemed to cling to its skin and mottled red flowers. Its lips curled back to reveal three-inch-long fangs. There was no trace of humanity in its body. It was lean and wolf-like, and it had burning red eyes.

The woman's eyes turned red, and she opened her mouth to reveal sharp fangs. Jenny could still hear her friends in the park, their laughter far away. The night turned bitter and threatening. The wind picked up, and the trees bent.

"Why are you doing this?" Jenny asked them. Tears were running down her face and she was heavily panting her eyes wide open in fear. The sound of crunching and bones filled her ears. Their bodies changed. Grew. Their bones cracking, their skin stretching and pulling. Both young men had dropped to the ground, their faces collapsing into teeth and the girl's eyes had turned blood red. The two men stood up and growled. The girl smiled devilishly at her, revealing razor-sharp fangs. Her dress dissolved, and the wind picked up.

The tree's leaves rustled, the grass bending toward the sky. The sky was still red, and the sound of a scream pierced her ears. Jenny felt sick, and her head throbbed. She was sweating and dizzy. The world was spinning.

On the ground, Leon writhed, popping bones out of his skin. His head ruptured, gore splattering down his body. Upon his head grew a long, snaking snout. Leon's hair fell out in clumps and his skin turned black, like a shadow.

"Run!" Leon snarled.

Jenny heard a voice in her head. She could not tell if it was her own thoughts or the creatures.

"You are not ready."

"I don't want this!" Jenny yelled, tears running down her face.

A dark shadow formed around Leon and his friend, and their bodies slowly moved lower to the ground. The woman in the red dress stood next to them with a grim expression on her face. A crackling sound came from the woods, followed by a rustling of leaves.

"You have been marked."

"You can't have her!" Leon growled back.

"I can take her from you!" the shadow said.

"No!" Leon turned around and picked Jenny up off the ground, holding her above his head. "I will take her from you!"

As he jumped backward, Leon's body changed. It was as if something had struck him, but no one had approached him. The wind seemed to catch at his coat and pull it tighter against his skin as if it were thickening. His clothes bunched up and seemed oddly rigid as if they had become armor. His face hardened. He looked like a stranger.

"You can't have her!" he screamed again, his voice half human and half the snarl of a beast.

Jenny felt hot, sticky, and dirty. She was weak and woozy, and her head felt like someone had hit her with a shovel. She looked over at Leon and the three other figures standing in a triangle on a patch of grass. The moon was red, and it was slightly larger than usual. She felt helpless—this thing was too powerful for her to fight.

The young woman in the red dress turned around and walked towards Jenny. Jenny was screaming and holding onto Leon's neck. The two tall guys ran forward and grabbed his arms, but he shook them off with ease. He stood up and started walking through the woods with the shadow following behind him. It was getting closer to Jenny, and she could see its long, black fingernails.

Jenny became hazy. Everything was blurry as if she were watching a movie. Everything around her seemed to stretch and twist upon itself. She watched as the men stepped on the trees and felt the branches of the trees snap beneath the soles of their boots. Covered in dirt and blood, the skinny kid stared at her with his cold, dark eyes and licked his thin lips. A long, red tongue darted out of his mouth and tasted the air. She watched him lick his cracked lips again before she smelled the earthy stench of rot coming off his breath.

The dark blue sky filled with black clouds that swirled angrily, blocking out the sun. Suddenly, the skies opened, and torrential rain came pouring down, pummeling the earth with heavy drops. The wind howled and voices shouted in the distance.

"Jenny? Where are you?"

Her legs gave way, and she collapsed to the ground.

She was lying on her back, looking up at the dark sky with water pelting her face. The branches of the trees intertwined above her, forming a canopy. She turned her head, the wet grass sticking to her cheek, and saw a man standing over her. He wore a black hooded sweatshirt, black jeans, and black boots. His face was completely black, with no features. His eyes glowed red.

He leaned in and said, "You're not ready."

A beast moved in front of her. She could hear the low guttural growl that was coming from its throat. Fire billowed up from the ground as the creature's eyes glowed red. Pulling back its mouth, showing blood-soaked razor-sharp teeth, it let out a deafening howl.

She could see the outline of people running towards her. "Jenny?!" they shouted.

"Go away!" she cried with what little strength she had left.

The beast continued to howl, and Jenny heard the screams of her friends in the distance. Two of the creatures charged toward the voices. They pounced on her friends. Suddenly her friends stopped screaming. Jenny could hear bones breaking and cracking. She could hear the smacking of teeth, the tearing of flesh, and the cracking of bones. She could hear the pain, sorrow, and terror in her friends' voices, which were muffled by thick gurgling sounds.

Just beyond the circle, Jenny could see Charlotte being torn apart. Her friend lay on the ground with blood and grey matter pouring down her face. They cracked her lower jaw open, and they split her skull wide. Another creature joined the scene, ripping out Charlotte's intestines and holding them up in the air. It stretched its mouth back, and it growled with a deep sound that rumbled from its chest and penetrated the souls of all who heard it. The creature held the intestines up like a trophy and howled with joy. A fine spray of blood splattered across Jenny's face, rich with red oxygen and full of life.

Jenny watched a beast rip the intestines out of Charlotte's body as it collapsed. Its body twitched uncontrollably. Above her, the dark sky opened, and rain poured down in buckets. The rain ran into her mouth and stung her eyes. Slowly, the light in the forest faded away. Jenny covered her mouth, trying to hold in her scream. Standing on hind legs, a beast rose from the woods and held Charlotte's intestines aloft for all to see, ripping them apart until there was nothing left. They continued to feast on Jenny's friends, ripping and tearing at them. One creature ran over to Jenny and bit into her arm.

A beast's snarling face was inches from hers, and its teeth tore at the flesh of her shoulder. It pulled her into the woods by her blood-soaked shirt, and she screamed. She could hear the high-pitched sound of her own voice, but the forest was spinning around her, the red oaks and green maples swirling into dervishes. Her vision blurred, and the world became red. Whether her eyes were closed or open, she could not see any better. The forest was dark, and then it was red, then it was black. A carpet of leaves swirled at her feet and ran past her eyes. A candle flickered in the distance, a single candle that cast long, dancing shadows around it.

Rachel was running towards her. Her gait was lopsided, and she was holding onto her side and crying. She pushed her long brown hair out of her face. She had a look of desperate determination on her face, and she was screaming and crying as she limped toward Jenny. Rachel tried to speak, but the blood that poured from her mouth strangled her words and hindered her breathing. She fell forward into Jenny's arms. Blood oozed out from around Rachel's fingers and from a deep cut on her side. Her eyes stared blankly at Jenny while the life left her body.

Rachel slowly collapsed to the ground, her body slack until she was a pile of skin and bones. She was in the center of a circle of monsters who were tearing her body apart. They pulled off her skin, her tendons snapping as they wrenched them from her body. Jenny could hear Rachel's face being ripped from its skull. She could hear the rupturing of tendons, the popping of bones, and the fabric-like sound of skin ripping from muscle. Jenny felt ill, but she turned her head and stared straight at the gore. She could see Rachel's ribs exposed, hanging loosely in front of her chest cavity. The monsters had torn her face off and lay on the ground next to where Rachel's head had once been.

The creatures attacking Rachel's body turned and looked at Jenny. The beasts climbed on top of each other until they formed one enormous creature. It rose into the air and then it fell back down to the ground. The creature screamed and Jenny heard cracking bones, as though it was building its body from the bones of her friends. The creature turned to Jenny with eyes that burned hungrily with a dark light. It opened its dark lips, revealing teeth like black needles.

Jenny turned her head away. She did not see anyone. She squeezed her fists tight and spun her head back. The wind whipped her hair into her face. It smelled like rain. A warm drop landed on her skin, and she wiped it away, looking for a place to take shelter from the storm. She saw the creature out of the corner of her eye, running towards her, its lips pulled back and a guttural, growling sound coming from its throat. It was going to eat her, rip her apart, and feast on her flesh just like it had done her friends. She screamed and held her face, covering her eyes.

Jenny closed her eyes momentarily and let out a quick gasp. She couldn't see a single soul upon opening her eyes. Her hair was still being whipped harshly into her face, stinging her eyes, and blocking her view. Raindrops cascaded down her skin. The first drop she wiped away, but another followed, and she felt its warmth on her wrist. The storm was closing in, but she couldn't see it or hear it outside the whistling of the wind through the trees. She felt a cold drop land on her cheek, but when she looked up to see where it had come from, the drops were gone. Yet that warmth lingered on her skin, and she wiped the second drop away with a shudder.

FOURTEEN

The phone startled the sheriff from his daydreaming, and he fished it out of his shirt pocket. Madison could hear the whole thing on her end.

"Yeah," he said, "Yeah, I know, we're on our way now. No, no, no, get the fire department ready."

"We may have a semi-major problem in the park," he said.

"Bunch of kids at the park. People have heard screaming. Probably just drinking and getting their stupid on, but we should check it out anyway. It's on Main Street. I'll take my truck. Meet me there?"

"Another fight?"

"No, it's not clear. I'm going to go check it out."

"Alright, I'll follow you."

The sheriff got into his truck and turned on his lights. Red and blue lights blazed forth from the roof of the old Ford truck, and the sirens sang their song of warning. Madison got into her car and followed. They flashed as the sheriff turned down this street, then pulled left into that alley, stopping for nothing. Bicycles, baby carriages, mothers with strollers, dogs, cats - all fell aside to let him pass. The sheriff drove through the stop signs at intersections, drove over speed bumps and twin streetlights that were installed too close together, and swerved around mailboxes. He drove through rain puddles splashing through streams that were rushing across the road in small rivers.

They were not going fast, but they weren't going slow either. They drove through the streets, Madison following the sheriff's lead closely.

He jolted the truck hurriedly through the streets, not bothering to use his turn signals, while Madison carefully watched, and then followed. He pitted the truck like he owned the road, yet Madison stayed back, following safely. The engine roared as the car hit each bump in the road, and she kept her foot pressed firmly on the gas pedal.

The sheriff hit the last bump in the road before the park, and he started driving slower, pulling over to the side of the road. Madison pulled up behind him and honked her horn.

She walked up to the park and listened. Parked under a shady tree was the sheriff's patrol car. The sheriff was talking on his radio, the radio squawking and hissing in her ear. She walked over to the car and leaned against it, listening to him talk.

"All right, get a unit over there and get them out of there. I don't care how you do it, just get them out of there."

"Yeah, yeah, yeah."

The sheriff turned around and noticed Madison. Shaking his head, he laughed, and she shrugged.

"What are they doing?" she asked.

"Well, it looks like there is a fight."

Approaching the park, they heard a scream. It was a scream of terror and pain, and both started running towards it. The sound of growling, the sound of another scream, the sound of something feral and primal, and then dead silence. The smell of death, both sweet and sour, and the sound of something else in the distance. A man screamed in terror and pain, a cry that was cut short by a gurgle as something untamed leaped from the shadows. Dragging its prey into the darkness to feed, it turned its head towards them, sniffing the air.

"What was that?" Madison asked breathily.

"I don't know, but all I can say is, god help them if we're too late."

The crowd of teenagers was fleeing, their screams fading into the background. A huge, grey wolf-like beast had emerged from the trees and was attacking one group. The creature's claws were the size of human hands, sharp enough to tear through flesh, and its fangs large enough to break bones without a problem. Eyes blacker than any human soul stared from a face that seemed all too human as it stalked closer.

The sheriff had never seen anything so horrible. The beast rooted through the forest, dragging the bodies around like rag dolls. There was nothing left but reddened streaks on the ground, and a flattened section of flora where it had dug its claws into the dirt to pull them deeper into the woods.

"I am getting my shotgun," the sheriff said. "You get the rifle."

Madison nodded quickly and grabbed the rifle from beside the tire. They both ran and knelt behind a bench in the middle of the park. For a moment, Madison felt overwhelmed by their newness. The first time they gave her a gun was when she was nine when her father took her to the shooting range for her birthday. She had never been comfortable with guns, but she had spent so many hours getting used to them that she could now shoot better than most men. She had never fired at a living thing before, but she knew this was only because she had never had the opportunity. At least now she would get her chance.

"What the hell is that thing?" she asked.

"I wish I knew," the sheriff said. "I really do."

Picking up the radio, he keyed it twice, calling all units from other nearby counties. He waited through three clicks and then repeated his message, his voice as sharp and even as a handsaw. He listened again to the crackle of the radio, listening for the confirmation of his fellow officers. After creating a loop, he turned to Madison and got ready for the shot.

"You ready?" he asked.

"Yes."

Running towards the wooded part of the park with his shotgun in his hands, the sheriff watched as the beast dragged body after body into the woods with its claws. He could feel something in the pit of his stomach. It was a feeling of dread, a feeling of something terrible, and it was deep within him.

The sheriff raced towards the woods, and Madison followed. He turned around and saw that Madison was still there, her eyes wide with fright. Another howl rang out, and it was close, closer than it had ever been before.

"Let's go," he said.

Worse, the fog was getting thicker and thicker. He could just barely make out the line between what was fog and what was air. His foot hit a rock, and he tumbled and fell, but he was back up in an instant. Once he got his footing, he was back, running as fast as he could move. The fog obscured even the grass beneath his feet. Worse, his footing was unsure. He stumbled again and almost fell but caught himself and kept on running.

The sheriff ran through the fog, his breath coming in ragged pants. His heartbeat pounded in his ears. In the quiet between heartbeats, he heard the pounding of the wolf creature's paws running after him. He could see their shadows darting through the fog behind him. As close as they were, it sounded like there were a dozen of them. The beast's howls were so loud that they hurt his ears and made his legs twitch. His foot got caught on a dead branch and he fell to the ground. One of the wolf creatures landed right next to him and its horrible, hot breath blew over his face. He grimaced and shut his eyes, preparing for the bite that would take him down into the darkness he was descending through.

It howled, turned, and ran away into the fog. When it was gone, not just from his sight but from the fog, he saw it. A body lay there, torn to pieces, his limbs bitten off and

J.C. MOORE

ripped to shreds. The skull was crushed in, and flesh and gore smeared across its face.

"Oh god," the sheriff uttered, "Oh god."

"Where?" Madison asked. "I don't see anything."

"There," he said, and he pointed straight ahead, "Over there."

A thick canopy of leaves blocked out the moonlight. Madison could see nothing. She couldn't even make out the faint glow of her cell phone to light the way. It was as if she were blind.

"Look, I can barely see anything. How are you going to see anything?"

"Shhhh," he said, "They're here. I can feel them. They're close. Just be ready."

He listened, trying to focus on the sounds, his ears straining to pick them out from the sound of the wind rustling through the leaves and the insects buzzing in the thickets. He couldn't feel them, only hear them. The sound of the monsters was nearby, close enough for him to raise his head and try to look at them. Then it was far away, and then it was nearby again. His heart raced.

"What do you think that means?" she asked in a whisper.

"It means we have to be ready for them," he replied in a hushed tone. "Whatever happens, we have to keep each other safe."

Madison's heart leaped into her throat. She couldn't see a thing. She couldn't move. For a split second, she entertained the idea of shooting her way out, but they were too close. One shot could mean death for all of them. The darkness pressed on her eyes like two huge hands, and she

182

sank to the ground, waiting for a knife to plunge between her shoulders. The darkness was suffocating, and she could barely breathe.

"I can't hear anything. What do you hear? Tell me what you hear."

"I hear them," he said. "They're not that far away. Get ready, aim for the head."

"Okay," she said, "I am ready."

"Good, I'm ready too."

"I don't know how the hell you're going to shoot from here," he said, "But you'd better be ready. The things are getting closer and closer."

She glanced down at her weapon, her mind questioning her quick decision. She adjusted the telescopic sight, and the crosshairs were on target. The weapon would catch any movement, enabling her to kill if needed. The gun felt totally alien in her hands. Like she had never used a weapon before, and she did not know how to deal with this situation.

He could hear them, and they were getting closer.

"They're getting closer," he said to Madison.

A clicking noise came from nearby, and Madison got ready. Her muscles flexed and relaxed, repeatedly, like a machine learning its task. She strained her ears to pick up the slightest sound. All they could do was wait. They waited for what seemed like eternity and then Madison heard a low growl off to the left of their position.

"Oh God, there," the sheriff said, pointing.

Madison could barely see it. She could just make it out—a shimmer of darkness, dancing around her through the fog, then disappearing. It was close, and it was ready to pounce. But then it was gone. The creature was gone from sight, and it was gone from the fog. It was toying with them.

"I don't know where it went," he said. "I can't see it."

The sheriff listened, and she listened, and he watched, and she watched. The fog was thick, and the woods were thick as well, and all they could do was wait, watch, and listen. Everything was quiet, as the air was still. She turned the rifle loose in her grip; it slipped under the pressure of her sweaty palms, letting the barrel drag across the trunk of the tree. Using one hand to hold her binoculars to her eyes and one hand to hold on to the trunk of the tree. There was nothing more to do than to wait.

"I still don't hear a sound," Madison said lowly.

"How can you not hear anything?" he asked.

"I don't know what I'm supposed to be hearing," she said.

There was a rustling in the trees, and the leaves began moving. The sheriff pointed his shotgun, and Madison got ready to shoot.

Suddenly, the creature jumped at him, and Madison squeezed the trigger without hesitation. She fired off a shot, and the bullet hit the creature. It stopped in midair and squealed in pain. The sheriff then fired his own shot, the bullet impacted on the creature's chest, and knocked it back. The sheriff reloaded his shotgun and he fired one more shot. It landed squarely between the creature's eyes, and it fell to the ground, dead.

The two were silent, and both stared at the creature. "What the hell was that?" Madison whispered.

"I don't know," he responded quietly.

They stood there, terrified by a sound they could not quite identify. It was a woman, but her wail was made from a thousand voices, each in agony and despair. A voice that could have come from the depths of hell. No, it wasn't her voice screaming; she was weeping, sobbing, and she had not just one voice, but many. Dozens of animals raced past them, heading deeper into the forest.

"Point toward a clearing in the woods," the sheriff said. "I'm going to head towards the scream."

Terrified, with adrenaline racing through his veins, he crept through the woods. His heart pounded almost painfully against his chest. Sweat and dirt burned his eyes, but he did not want to wipe them; he couldn't lose sight of his enemy. He followed the wails, and he followed the rustling until he reached the edge of a clearing in the woods. The clearing was massive, and the fog covered everything. All he could see was darkness. He squinted his eyes, trying to make out details; trying to find a target to aim at. He saw a black silhouette moving in the distance. His ears strained to hear over the pounding of his own heartbeat in his ears.

The smell was the first thing that he noticed. It was a smell of death, a smell of decay and putrefaction. He could smell the wildlife surrounding the clearing, and then he saw it. The moonlight pierced through the dense forest and shone into an enormous clearing. Each twig, leaf, and blade of grass bathed in the clear, white moonlight. The sheriff could see it.

"Oh god," he muttered only to himself.

The bodies of boys and girls, men and women, their arms ripped off, their skin shredded into tiny pieces, their bodies torn to pieces, their heads crushed and broken, covered the clearing. The damp earth drank up the blood that poured from the unmoving bodies.

The sheriff followed the mud path through the woods. The dull crunch of his shoes on the ground and the soft rustle of his pants were the only sounds he heard. His hands were sweaty, and his palms were slippery on the gun's grip, but he kept following. Then he saw them. A young woman was lying sprawled on the ground, her long brown hair fanned out around her. The ground rumbled.

Three creatures, tall and slender like giraffes, with coarse brown hair on their faces and backs, paced around the prone woman. In the circle, another woman stood in a red dress holding a scythe. Her expression was pinched, and her arms were folded across her chest. Her blonde hair had come loose from its braid, and tendrils flailed into the air. The creatures were on their hind legs and had to lean forward to reach the woman lying down. She squealed and covered her face with her hands. One beast was sniffing at her hair, its sharp nose brushing against her earlobe and sniffing at her dark tresses. Its long tongue licked hungrily at her tender flesh.

The sheriff sat his gun across his knees, a familiar feeling but not exactly comfortable. Its normally warm barrel was cool to the touch, and the weight of the gun on his knees was reassuring. The sheriff aimed it at the beast on the left that was rearing back its horse-like head to bite.

FIFTEEN

S truggling for air, Jenny could smell the stench of rot-
ting flesh. She felt the beast's claws cut her skin and
tear her flesh. There was an icy feeling rushing through her
body, as If ice cold water was being injected into her veins.
The creature's head, twisted in an expression of rage, was
right in front of her. It had long, black, lifeless hair and
cold, black eyes. Pouring from its wide-open mouth was
a tongue that was long, black, and forked like a snake's
tongue.

"No" Jenny screamed. "No!" she continued to cry. "No!
No! No! No! No!"

Jenny wept. She couldn't control the sobs that were
welling up inside of her. She could no longer hear the
sounds of her friends being killed. All she could hear were
her own cries, the sound of her own misery, like someone
was calling for help and she couldn't answer.

They turned to look at Jenny and the woman in the red
dress walked towards her, dagger raised. "You are not ready

yet," it said. Its voice was like a whisper and a shout, a clap of thunder that was followed by a groan of pain.

Jenny could hear the voice in her head again, gentle: "You are not ready. Come back to me."

A warm liquid was running down her leg, and she felt herself getting light-headed. There was a loud bang, like a gunshot, and the creature howled in pain. She could hear sirens in the distance and then a car door slamming shut. The lights blinded her.

There was another loud whooshing sound, and she could feel a warm liquid splattering on her chest. There was an explosion, and Jenny could feel the ground shake.

She heard someone shouting, "Everybody out! Now!"

The beast was moving faster now, dragging her by the legs deeper into the woods. Her eyes watered, and she felt the dirt climb up her forehead and back and nestle in her hair. Her body was limp, and completely numb. She could feel the ground vibrating. There was a smoldering tire on the ground and a black truck with its headlights on.

She could feel nothing except the burn of her skin as it dragged her across the ground.

Another gunshot reverberated through the air, followed by a howl of agony. The creature holding her by the legs dropped her body to the ground. Jenny could see a large red stain on its chest. She watched as it slowly turned around and lumbered off. It growled and disappeared into the woods. Jenny could hear the sirens getting louder and the sound of tires on wet pavement.

She felt a cool breeze on her skin, and she heard a car door opening and closing. The sound of someone crying echoed through the trees. She heard the faint sounds of feet running through grass and she felt the whoosh of a skirt as someone ran by.

"Jenny," the voice called. "Jenny"

Loud, distinct sounds of a vehicle engine approached. The low growl sounded like a huge woodchipper chewing up trees, rocks, and pebbles. A crunching of leaves and metal, small rock stones—then a sudden stop.

A bright light shone over Jenny, hurting her eyes. She squinted and looked up to see a fire truck. Rain was pouring down on Jenny like a waterfall. It crept down her cheeks and slid down her back, making her shiver beneath her warm blanket. When it touched the pine needles and cool dirt of the forest floor, the water changed from a pure white mist to a deep brown. The tree branches rustled and swayed in the wind, their leaves flapping like the wings of crows desperate to take flight. A figure was coming closer to her with a shotgun in their hands. They turned the figure around and there was a flash of red, followed by a loud bang. The creature fell to the ground, shaking its head as if trying to make sense of what had just happened.

"We have to get out of here! We have to go! NOW!" yelled a man's voice.

A man in his early fifties was dragging Jenny toward their vehicle. He held her by the arms and lifted her off the ground, and she whimpered. Her legs were useless. He grabbed her around the waist and threw her over his shoulder, but it was awkward, as if he had never carried a person before. He tried again, but she fell to the ground. The man sighed and ran over to her and lifted her off the ground again and threw her over his shoulder without even looking down. He ran over to the truck and opened the passenger door. The rusty hinges screamed in protest as he swung the door open, but he ignored them and tossed Jenny into the cab of the car as gently as he could manage in his state of urgency.

It was the town sheriff. Jenny groaned, "It moved."

The sheriff slammed the door shut and ran to the driver's side of the truck. He jumped in, slammed the door, and turned the key. The engine roared to life. The truck jolted forward, crushing something on the ground. He slammed on the brakes just as the fire truck and police car pulled up behind him. He looked behind him and saw a deformed creature with a mangled head and blood oozing from its eyes and nose. The sheriff slammed on the gas and the truck lurched forward.

The sheriff turned around and saw the beast lunging toward the back window. It was too late for the sheriff to hit the brakes. The beast slammed into the back window, shattering it. He fell unconscious immediately when his head bounced off the steering wheel. The truck was in neutral, and it rolled backwards.

Jenny opened her eyes and saw the beast's hand reaching through the broken back window. It dragged her painfully through the shattered glass after grabbing her by the neck. She felt the chilly air on her back, and then she was flying. She landed on the ground, face first. It rolled her over, and swiped at her stomach with its claws, and she could feel the fluid oozing out of her stomach.

Her body was cold and unresponsive. She forced herself to roll over and saw the truck roll backwards, crushing a beast again and again against a tree. She saw the sheriff's head bounce off the steering wheel, but he was still out cold. The truck was still rolling backwards, but the beast was now gone. She thought it must be dead. The sound of a branch breaking made her turn her head toward the sound.

She saw the fire truck pull up behind the truck, and a firefighter jumped out. He grabbed the sheriff and dragged him towards him. Another firefighter jumped out of the fire truck and ran towards Jenny.

She was lying on her side, and she felt a warm liquid running down her leg.

"Okay, sweetie. Come on. Help me out." The firefighter lifted her into the air and secured a mask to her face. It was cold, and they attached an oxygen tank to it.

The firefighter heaved her up over his shoulder and started running towards the fire truck, his boots splashing through the water. He held her tight with one arm and the other hung limp by his side, his hand white-knuck-led around his service weapon. He set her down in the seat next to the sheriff, who was unconscious. Two other firefighters were working on the sheriff. He could hardly endure their torture, his body shaking and bubbling with thick spit as they worked to save him.

The firefighter pulled a blanket over Jenny, but it did not feel warm or soothing at all. Just cold. The sirens wailed. The police and fire radios were crackling. She could hear the sheriff groan. She could hear the firefighters talking about the sheriff. Something about a heart attack and a stroke.

She could still hear gunshots and howling, but it was faint.

She could hear the firefighter talking to the sheriff: "You're going to be okay," he reassured.

Jenny tried to move her arms and legs, but was unsuccessful, and she could feel a tingling sensation in her body. She felt like she was slipping into a deep sleep.

She could hear the firefighter talking to the sheriff again. "I've got to get you out of here. We need to go now," he said. "I'm going to put you in the back of our truck, okay? We are going to take you to the hospital. You're going to be okay. Stay with me. Stay with me."

The sheriff groaned.

Jenny could feel the firefighter grab the sheriff's arm and pull him up. He slammed the door shut and then ran back to his truck.

A few minutes later, the firefighter returned with a stretcher and worked on the sheriff again. The other firefighters were loading up their gear.

The firefighter looked at Jenny and said, "I'm sorry, sweetie."

Jenny squeezed her eyes shut, and she saw flashes of light and darkness. The sirens were getting louder, and she could feel the ground vibrating. The noises in her head drowned the voices of the firefighters out. She could feel her heart pounding in her chest. A trail of blood trickled down her cheek and into her ear. When she opened her eyes again, the firefighter was looking at her. His face was red and sweaty, and he was wheezing. He was straining to keep the plasma bag above her. She could see a bright light in the distance.

Jenny could feel the warmth of a blanket over her shoulders, and she could see the bright red flashing lights of the ambulance. She could hear the firefighter and the paramedics talking urgently.

There was a loud crunching sound, and the ground shook. The firefighter and the paramedics looked over towards the tree line. They could hear sirens in the distance and a howling sound. The sirens were getting louder and closer. They saw the bright lights of the police car pulling up behind the ambulance. A white light was shining on the tree line.

Another figure stood at the edge of the parking lot. It was a woman. Her hands hung in front of her belt, by her badge. The face was merely a shadow behind the brim of the cap. She looked at her partner, who was now being loaded on the stretcher into the ambulance. She looked at a parked car that was flipped upside down and burning but was still recognizable as being mostly intact. The headlights of another police officer's cruiser, which had caught on fire, illuminated all of this. The shadow seemed to stare into the woods for a moment, then turned and walked closer to them.

The woman looked at the ground and saw a massive pool of blood.

As she was walking back towards the ambulance, she saw two beasts appear out of the tree line. She screamed, "THERE! THERE!" They dropped to all fours and charged.

Her gun was slippery with sweat as she drew it. She tried to steady her hand. She squeezed the trigger when she heard another gunshot. As she turned around, the other police officer had his gun drawn. The first one flew back and landed hard and ran. The second beast fell to the ground. She could hear a loud bang and she turned back around. The first one was gone.

She heard another loud bang and turned around and saw the second beast struggling to get back to its feet. Covered in blood, it let out a massive howl and then collapsed.

The paramedic was looking at the deputy with a stunned look on his face. "Are you okay?"

"Just take care of the sheriff," she said.

The paramedic nodded and worked on the sheriff again.

The paramedic could hear the sheriff groaning. He could feel the sheriff's warm blood on his gloves. The paramedic heard footsteps behind him, and another paramedic was standing there. The new paramedic worked on Jenny. She could feel her body relaxing.

She could hear the paramedic asking the sheriff how he was feeling. The paramedic's hands were warm. She could feel her body tingling, like she went swimming for too long and her body was getting cold.

The sheriff was unconscious. The paramedic felt his neck and said, "He's got a pulse and he's breathing."

The police car's radio crackled, and they could hear, "Officer down. Officer down!"

SIXTEEN

M adison watched as the creature charged her again. She could see its bright blue eyes and its long, sharp claws. The beast was howling and snarling. She fired another shot into its head. Its head jerked back, and it stumbled and fell to the ground. She could see the creature struggling to get back to its feet. It lowered its head and charged. She fired her last shot. This time, it struck the beast's shoulder, and it fell to the ground with a loud thud. The beast was still. Madison began running towards it. She could hear it howl and she could see it struggling to get up. She drew her holstered pistol and fired a final shot into its head. It fell back to the ground, now completely motionless.

Stepping over its body, she continued running. She heard gunshots again. She saw a bright orange light in the distance. As she ran, the gunshots grew louder. She recognized the sound and knew it was the firefighter. She could see the fire truck and the ambulance.

There was a loud bang. She felt the ground shake and heard another beast let out a howl. It was not even ten feet from her. Screaming, she raised her gun. It charged toward her. She dropped to the ground, and it flew over her and continued running. She got up when she heard another gunshot. It flew backward, taking down several trees in its wake.

She heard a clicking sound, and she looked down and saw the magazine was empty.

Before she could reload, the creature was back on its feet. It charged toward her, snarling and growling. She ran. Glancing back towards the creature as it was running and saw the bright light of the ambulance. She was almost there. It was getting closer, and she could hear its growling fill her mind.

Heading toward the ambulance and she ran to the back door. She tried to open it, but it was stuck. The door swung open as she slammed her shoulder into it. It lunged at her as she jumped into the back of the ambulance. She fell to the ground as the beast jumped over her and spun to face her.

It was growling and snarling at her. She shivered and felt her body getting cold with fear. She heard it howl again. It was trying to get back to its feet. She then heard another gunshot. The beast fell back to the ground and began crawling towards the ambulance.

She got up as it struggled towards her. She jumped over it and ran towards the front of the ambulance. The door swung open after she slammed her hand against the button. She jumped into the back of the ambulance behind the sheriff. The sheriff was lying on the stretcher. She could see the paramedic leaning over him. The sheriff's face was flushed and covered in sweat.

"Stay with me, stay with me," the paramedic said.

Madison saw the paramedic shiver and a shiver ran down her spine as well. She turned around and saw the creature crawling towards them. She could hear the paramedic saying, "Stay with me, stay with me."

It was roaring, and she could hear its claws scraping against the metal walls.

She spun around and saw the sheriff's shotgun lying unused on the ground. She grabbed it hastily and turned back around. The beast was running towards the sheriff. She aimed the shotgun at its head. She fired. It fell straight down like a tree being felled by a woodsman's ax. She heard the thing struggling to get back to its feet. She fired a second shot. Its head jerked to the side and a large amount of blood poured from its head. She fired a third shot. Its head exploded, splattering blood over her face.

A woman suddenly appeared from the trees, almost floating above the ground in a long, flowing red dress. Her blonde hair hung down below her waist. Blood dripped from her chin onto her white collar and coat. Her left hand held a huge scythe which was dripping with a river of deep, red blood. She lowered herself until she was hovering just above the ground and looked up towards Madison. She turned her head to the side and spat out a piece of tongue. Madison could see that she was missing several teeth. The woman's tongue was long and pink. She noticed Madison aiming the shotgun at her.

The woman growled, her voice growing bestial as her body shifted. She had pale skin and cracks on her face that resembled an old porcelain doll. Two small fangs jutted out of her lower jaw and her mouth grew long, stretching down to her chin. Her eyes shrank into a cold flatness as they sank into her head, which shifted backward on her neck so that they turned upside down. The woman lifted her blade and swung it at Madison. The blade sliced through the air like a snake and aimed straight for Madison's head.

Madison raised her gun and took aim. She squeezed the trigger and watched in horror as the bullet bored a hole through the woman's head and left a gaping wound behind. The woman stumbled back, dropping the blade as she did so. She looked at Madison with cold indifference as she turned her right side up again. The bullet had not stopped her at all, only slowed her down a bit. She opened her mouth wide, her teeth shifting into fangs. She lunged at Madison, moving quickly despite the gaping wound in her head.

"You bitch!" the woman screamed.

Another shot rang out. The woman's head jerked to the side, and she stumbled, her momentum carrying her forward. Madison watched as the woman's head slid off her shoulders and fell to the ground. The woman staggered back. She looked at Madison and blood spouted from the wound. Madison watched as the woman fell to her knees. The woman looked at Madison and their eyes met for a moment. The woman's eyes were cold and empty.

Madison felt numb. The shotgun was heavy in her hands. She thought she was going to throw up, and she felt dizzy.

Saliva was dripping from her mouth as her heart was drumming painfully in her chest.

Panting, breathless, and moving as quickly as her legs could carry her, Madison ran to the ambulance and threw open the doors. Her knees banged against metal and her boots slid across the polished floor. A thud hit the top of it, rocking it back and forth. The creature was here. She slammed the doors shut. Her heart beating quickly in her chest, she ran toward the front of the ambulance. There was a loud bang, louder than any gun she had heard fired before, behind her. The doors shook violently as part of their metal buckled inward beneath a strength no human possessed.

"Move!" she screamed at the paramedic sitting in the seat.

Madison jumped into the driver's seat and put the key into the ignition. Another beast banged on the sides and roof of the ambulance, howling and snarling. She tried to turn the ignition, but there was no response. She tried again. The creature thrashed on the doors and the side windows. She tried the ignition again, muttering quiet curse words as it banged on the driver's window. The window cracked. She tried the ignition again. The creature banged on the door continuously. As it banged on the driver's window again, the door buckled and shook. The glass shattered as it punched an enormous hole through the window.

It now had her by the hair, pulling her toward the window. She reached for her revolver on her hip and tried to pull it out of the holster. The holster would not release it.

It had a tight grip on her hair as she tried to pull back. She tried to use her other hand and pull its hand from her hair, but it was too strong. Finally freeing her revolver, she fired three times. Three red welts stood out on its dark skin, like red paint on black velvet. It released her hair and fell to the ground. Where the bullets had hit it, its blood stained its dark skin a dark crimson. It growled a low grating sound that rumbled in the back of its throat.

She slammed the door open and ran out of the ambulance. Her footsteps beat a tattoo on the ground as she ran. Only one bullet remained in her gun. A bullet hit it in its open mouth and blew out the back of its head. As it fell to the ground, it spasmed violently, as if it was convulsing. It tried to stand but collapsed like a marionette with its strings cut. It tried to crawl away, but her eyes followed it, following its actions as if they were a script. She quickly reloaded, raised the gun, braced it with two hands, and fired a single shot. The bullet hit the creature in the back of the head, jerking its head forward with the impact.

"Die you fucker!" she screamed.

Raising her gun again and closing one eye, she focused her aim on its head. She exhaled softly and squeezed the trigger. The gun barked out and kicked sharply against her shoulder. The beast staggered under the hit and roared angrily. Its head jerked forward, spraying black blood from its mouth. Its body swayed for a moment, and then it hit the ground with a heavy thud. She stood above it for a moment and watched as blood pooled out from under it. Its body twitched erratically as if it were still trying to escape and then came to a stop.

She ran back to the ambulance and threw open the doors.

She turned back towards the sheriff as he grabbed her hand and squeezed. She could hear the sheriff groaning and saying, "I'm going to be okay."

The paramedic prodded the IV bag and the sheriff groaned. He blinked and called out, "Madison?"

Madison smiled. As her body relaxed, she could feel herself being brought back to reality.

"Everything's going to be okay," she said, and tears ran down her cheeks as she spoke.

She looked down at the young woman lying by the sheriff. She was sobbing. Madison walked towards her and knelt beside her. She put her arm around the woman and cried with her.

Jenny turned to her; her brow furrowed with worry. "What is your name?" she asked her.

"Madison," she said.

"Thank you," Jenny said.

Madison then turned to the paramedic and said, "I'm done here. Get us moving."

A moment later, she heard the siren wail and felt the ambulance rumble to life. She could hear Jenny sobbing. Madison sat in the back, looking out the window through a red mist of tears. The ambulance lights cut through the darkness, sirens blaring loudly. Madison looked out the window at the shattered streets and the wreckage of fallen homes and businesses. She saw the familiar gas station. She looked at the young woman. The young woman looked up at her. She said something. Madison did not understand what she said. She wanted to ask her to repeat herself, but she was already drifting away, into a sea of darkness.

The moon cast a blood-red glow over the streets. She felt as if she were floating through a haze, moving in slow motion through a swirling dream, as a red haze of homes and businesses flashed past her window. She heard someone shout, "Clear." A crowd had gathered around the wreck. The ambulance was racing through the night. She heard Jenny sobbing beside her; distant and muffled, like drifting in space.

SEVENTEEN

The sheriff stirred, and Madison immediately tossed her magazine to the floor and looked up. She was sitting in a straight-backed chair, with her hands rested on the table. She had taken off her shoes. The floor was cold on the bottom of her feet. There was a Pepsi can on the table in front of her.

"Hey there," she said, "it looks like you decided to join us."

"Is that so?" asked the sheriff in a rasping voice. The tubes and oxygen mask attached to his face almost obscured it completely. "Here are the damn doctors again. They just won't leave me alone."

He waved his hand in irritation, but Madison's smile remained brightly on her face. The doctors spoke with each other and quickly left the room, closing the door behind them. Madison turned back to the sheriff. "Do you need anything?"

"A drink," said the sheriff.

"I thought you gave that stuff up."

"I did...sort of, but now it's really starting to piss me off."

"Really? Now, what do you need?"

"A big can of cola."

"You got it," said Madison, as she picked up her purse.

"How is she?" asked the sheriff.

"She's a strong girl. She'll make it."

"Can I see her?"

"I can try and get you clearance, but they're pretty strict. No one is supposed to see her."

"Please," he said, "I just want to see her."

"Okay," Madison said. "I'll ask."

"Thank you, Madison."

"Welcome, sir"

"What in the hell were those things?" he stuttered.

"Something sent straight from hell," she answered, still in disbelief.

Madison walked out of the room and down the hallway. She pushed open the door to the waiting room and walked in. Jenny was sitting in a chair, looking out of the window. She looked up at Madison, her eyes were red from crying. "Hi, Madison," she said.

"How is he doing?"

"He's going to be fine; he just needs rest."

"Can I see him?"

"Well, I have some good news for you," said Madison. "He's awake, and he'd like to see you."

"You are kidding me," Jenny said, raising her eyebrows slightly in surprise.

Madison shook her head. "No, he's been asking for you."

"He's been asking for me?"

"He's strong," Madison said. "He'll be okay."

"I can't believe it," Jenny said.

"So, you ready to go see him?"

"Yeah," Jenny agreed.

"Good, I'll go tell the doctor and we'll head up there."

"No, it's okay, I'll go myself."

She walked down the hallway to his room. Jenny knocked on the door and pushed it open. The sheriff was sitting up in his bed. "Hi, Jenny," he said. "It's good to see you again."

"Hi, Sheriff," she said.

"Please, call me Owen. Owen Cross."

"Alright then, Owen."

"I have some news and I need to ask you a favor."

"What is it?"

He turned to Jenny and said, "Jenny, I know you are upset, so I'll get right to the point. Madison and I are so sorry about what happened. We wish we had more information about the whole situation."

Madison then walked into the room and sat down in a plastic chair.

Jenny's eyes begun to well with tears. She wiped her nose with the back of her hand, smearing snot and tears down her face. Madison looked at her with concern.

"You know that none of this is your fault," Madison said.

"I thought that I was all alone, and then I realized that you were there too, " Jenny said in a shaky voice. Her breath caught in her throat, and she sobbed again.

"It's okay," Madison said, patting Jenny on her hand. "Take some deep breaths and try to relax."

"Oh God, Leon was one of those things, too. Is he dead?"

"Yes, I am sorry," Madison whispered.

"I'm sorry too," the sheriff said. "None of this makes any damn sense. This is beyond our knowing." There were tears in his eyes. For too long he had held back his tears because of his fear of making a mistake, his fear of being afraid. Madison saw all of this for the first time.

"He was so good to me," she said.

The sheriff let out a loud sigh.

"I wish that it wasn't like this," she said.

"I do too, Jenny. I just want you to know that if you ever need anything, please let me know."

"Can I see my father and my brother?" Jenny said to Madison.

"Yes, they are in the waiting room," Madison replied. "I'll go get them."

Madison found Jenny's father and brother in the waiting room. She took them back to the sheriff's room with and watched with a small smile as Jenny embraced her father and brother. Madison could see tears running down their cheeks.

"I'll let you guys be alone," Madison said. She paused for a moment before turning and walking out of the hospital and into the night.

The light was fading. Behind the horizon, the sun was no longer visible. The town that she loved seemed to have grown darker and more menacing. Walking to her cruiser parked in the hospital's lobby lot she had a distant look in her eyes as she looked up at the black sky. She could hear the familiar hum of a distant highway, as the lights from passing cars periodically broke the darkness. Madison sat in her car for a moment and watched the sun sink fully into the horizon. She put her car in gear and drove home.

Miles away from Madison, and miles away from anything else, just west of the old mines, the last sliver of sunlight was fading from the sky and into the horizon. The young couple sat on the beach, looking out over the lake, holding each other, staring at the sunset.

"This is beautiful," the man said as he wrapped his arms around his woman and kissed her on the cheek. She turned toward him and smiled. Her rounded face glowed with happiness.

He smiled. "I love you."

"I love you, too."

The chilly winds whistled off the lake and whipped around them. Gulls flew around their heads and circled the trees on the hill behind where they stood. They called out to each other. The gray-white clouds turned a deep red, like an approaching storm. It had been a long time since there had been a storm at night; he thought.

The moon rose in the sky and bathed the lake with its gentle, red glow. The waves threw themselves onto the shoreline in a long, flat line and calmed as they reached their destination, just as the sea always calmed after a storm. They were never rough or frantic, like an angry man's heart or soul. The sky above glowed as if it would burst into flames. It glowed like a fire on the horizon when the gasoline ignites and burns so brightly that it lights up everything around it.

From the perimeter of the woods surrounding the lake, there was a faint howl. The young woman looked over at the woods with a look of fear and confusion on her face. Her companion stood and shone a small flashlight toward the source of the noise, but only snuffed out whatever light lay inside him. She could see someone dressed in a long black cloak. It raised its bone-white finger and pointed it at them. Then the finger went to its lips, and it formed a single word.

"Shhhh."

AFTERWORD

I spent a lot of time in Morgantown, West Virginia as a kid, where my parents grew up. I wanted to revisit my memories of
it for this novel (on which it was extremely loosely based). It was a small town- *not so small anymore*- but I felt the closeness
of a community like that could threaten the novel's characters. I also wanted to include a little of my family's history in this town.

My grandfather worked in the coal mines-an unforgiving environment with long hours and hard labor.

The strength of the miners is legendary, and their sacrifices are also legendary. I wanted to capture some of the hardworking, honest nature of
small-town America and how people help each other and take care of each other's children. It is a tough life, but people take pleasure in their work.

Every day counts for something.

I hope I did the characters justice.

I am thankful for all the support and congratulations I received during the launch of this novel.

Yours in reading,

J.C.

June 2022

ABOUT AUTHOR

J.C. is a published songwriter, father, husband, IT guy by day – but also moonlights as a professional musician.

He reads anything from classics to modern literature and pulp but is particularly fond of horror and science fiction. He is a fan of movies and writing that allow for the expression of characters' inner lives, as well as the idea that there are good people in the world who embody qualities such as kindness, empathy, and compassion. J.C. lives in Upstate NY with his wife and his dog Archie.

Made in United States
Orlando, FL
30 June 2022

19291768R00133